FAWN IN THE FOREST

'OK,' said Mandy, straightening up and turning to face her dad. 'How long can Sprite go on without milk, Dad, before . . . ?' Mandy gulped, then bit her lip, unable to finish the question.

Mandy's parents were always honest with her. They never gave her false hopes. After all, as much as they tried to, they couldn't cure every single animal who came to them.

Now, Adam Hope stroked his beard thoughtfully as Mandy and James, their eyes large and anxious, waited for his reply.

'I don't really know,' Mr Hope replied slowly. 'But I think if she hasn't taken any milk by this time tomorrow . . . Well, the odds will be stacked pretty heavily against her. And then—' He broke off and looked meaningfully at Mandy.

LUCY DANIELS

Fawn

— *in the* —

Forest

Illustrations by Shelagh McNicholas

Hodder
Children's
Books

a division of Hodder Headline plc

Special thanks to Pat Posner
Thanks also to C. J. Hall, B.Vet.Med., M.R.C.V.S., for reviewing
the veterinary information contained in this book.

Text copyright © 1997 Ben M. Baglio
Created by Ben M. Baglio, London W6 0HE
Illustrations copyright © 1997 Shelagh McNicholas
Cover art copyright © 1997 Peter Warner

First published in Great Britain in 1997
by Hodder Children's Books

ISBN 0 340 68715 0

Typeset by Avon Dataset Ltd, Bidford-on-Avon, Warks

Printed and bound in Great Britain by
Cox & Wyman Ltd, Reading, Berks

Hodder Children's Books
a division of Hodder Headline plc
338 Euston Road
London NW1 3BH

One

Midsummer's Day! Mandy Hope thought as she opened her eyes and gazed round her sun-filled bedroom. It was the longest day of the year. And, according to Gran, anyone who believed in magic would hear the little folk singing today as they made preparations for their midnight festival.

Mandy chuckled as she heard someone singing in the garden below her open window. 'That's not one of the little folk,' she whispered to herself as she got out of bed. 'That's Dad!'

'*The sun has got his hat on . . .*' The words drifted up to Mandy as she padded round her bedroom. Chuckling softly to herself, she reached for the glass of water on her bedside table then tip-toed over to the window.

Peeping out, Mandy looked down at Adam Hope's back and watched for a moment as, in between singing, he popped wild garden strawberries into his mouth.

Mandy spread her fingers across the top of the glass, got it into position and waited . . . '. . . *The sun has got his hat on, and he's coming out to play*!' her dad sang happily. Then . . .

Mandy carefully tilted the glass and allowed a few drops of water to trickle through her fingers. *Drip . . . drip . . . drip . . .* Mandy bit her lip to keep from laughing as her dad's hand went to the top of his head and he looked up at the sky in amazement.

Then he swung round and looked up at Mandy's laughing face. 'Very funny,' he said with a wide grin of his own. 'Come on down and have some breakfast,' he added. 'I'll pick some more strawberries.'

'Couldn't you sleep? It's only half-past six. That's early even for you, Dad,' Mandy said a few minutes later as she joined him in the garden.

'I was called out to Burnside Farm,' replied Mr Hope. 'Don't worry, everything's all right,' he went on hastily, seeing the look of alarm on Mandy's face. 'Clover's first calf, a heifer, arrived safely an hour or so ago. It's a good job John Matthews called me though. Clover needed a bit of help. The calf is a whopper and she was lying awkwardly.'

'So you had to turn the calf before Clover could deliver her?' said Mandy.

'That's right. And once I'd managed to do that, Clover got on with the job quite nicely.' Mr Hope confirmed with a smile.

Mandy smiled too and squeezed her dad's arm, thinking happily how glad she was he and her mum were vets. They were her adoptive parents really; her own parents had died in a car crash too early for Mandy to remember them. Adam and Emily Hope were the best parents anyone could wish for and Animal Ark, in the Yorkshire village of Welford, was the best place in the world to live.

'Hey, you must be miles away,' teased Mr Hope. 'I've offered you this strawberry three times.'

'No, I was right here,' laughed Mandy,

popping the strawberry into her mouth.

'Well, you're a couple of early birds. Catching strawberries instead of worms, I see.' Emily Hope came up behind them and helped herself to a strawberry from her husband's palm.

'Morning, Mum,' said Mandy. 'I made myself wake up early. James and I are going picking elderflowers for Gran and I want to do my chores first.'

'Oh, yes, Gran's going to make elderflower lemonade for next month's WI Fete.' Mrs Hope nodded and helped herself to another strawberry.

'She's never made it before,' said Mandy. 'She heard the recipe on the radio and—'

'And that was that!' Mr Hope finished. 'I bet Gran was on the phone begging elderflowers straight away. Where are you going for them?'

'Miss Davy's,' replied Mandy. 'Gran says the elder trees in the Old School House garden are the best in Welford. But she also says the flowers should be picked early in the morning!' Mandy giggled. 'Poor James had already agreed to help me before Gran told us that!'

'Are you meeting him at Miss Davy's or is he coming here first?' asked Mrs Hope.

'He's coming here. I invited him for breakfast, Mum; that's all right isn't it? He's going to help me move the rabbits' hutch before we go. I want to put it more in the shade.'

'Good idea, Mandy,' said her dad. 'We've treated a few overheated animals this week and, according to the weather forecast, it's going to get hotter still.'

'Not the right sort of weather for a pancake breakfast then?' Mrs Hope teased. She knew Mandy and James could eat pancakes whatever the weather.

'Oh, yes please, Mum!' Mandy gave her a quick hug. 'I sort of hinted to James that there could be pancakes,' she admitted with a grin. 'I had to say *something* to make sure he'd get up early.'

'Well, I'll make pancakes if *you* make the residents' breakfasts!' bargained Mrs Hope.

'Done!' Mandy agreed promptly. She loved going into the residential unit and attending to the animals so sick they had to stay in Animal Ark for a few days.

'Nothing for Humphrey,' Mrs Hope told her. 'He's having his operation later this morning.'

Humphrey was a soulful-looking bloodhound. Mandy loved his crinkly forehead and long, silky ears. 'I won't give him anything to eat or drink,' Mandy assured her mum, 'but I'll give him an extra dose of TLC to make up for no breakfast.'

'Your tender loving care is one of our best medications,' said Mr Hope, ruffling Mandy's blonde hair. 'It works wonders.'

'So do hints about pancake breakfasts,' chuckled Mandy as the pinging of a bicycle bell heralded James's arrival.

'I'm off for a shower,' said Mr Hope after greeting James. 'It's my turn for Saturday surgery this morning.'

James liked animals as much as Mandy did; so he was more than happy to help in the residential unit before moving the rabbits' hutch.

'Is the giant gerbil from Geoff's pet shop still here?' he asked Mandy as they made their way inside.

'You'll hurt Joey's feelings if you call him a gerbil,' scolded Mandy. 'He's a Shaw's jird. But yes, he's still here. His tail's better, though. Geoff's coming to fetch him later on today.'

James walked over to the jird's cage. Joey was about the same size as a rat and he *did* look like a giant version of a gerbil. He was a browny-grey colour with big, dark brown eyes and long whiskers that twitched inquisitively when he saw James looking at him. His tail was long, too. An easy target for another jird to grab hold of and bite!

'What do jirds eat?' James asked Mandy.

'Mainly a mixture of seed and grains like gerbils,' Mandy replied. 'But jirds like fruit and vegetables, too. And they need a small amount of meat in their diet. Dad says they should have some tinned cat food or a few mealworms two or three times a week.'

'I suppose it's one of Joey's mealworm days and you're going to suggest that I might like to feed him?' James said with a grin. Mandy wasn't squeamish, but James knew that handling mealworms wasn't her favourite job.

'Wow, James! You're on top form for someone who got up so early,' Mandy said as her friend went over to the sink to scrub his hands.

'It's the thought of your mum's pancakes,' James told her, walking back to Joey's cage.

'You know,' he continued, lifting the animal out, 'I think jirds are even friendlier than their . . .' he grinned and lowered his voice to a whisper, '. . . than their gerbil cousins.'

'Yes,' agreed Mandy. 'They really enjoy being cuddled. Joey's irresistible. But don't spend too long petting him, James. We've got a lot to do before we go to Miss Davy's. Including eating pancakes!'

By half-past eight, James and Mandy were on their way. They'd decided to walk and took the short cut down the lane that led past the cottages behind the Fox and Goose.

'Now then, young miss, young sir,' Walter Pickard from the last cottage greeted them. 'Off to Eileen Davy's, are you?'

'Good morning, Walter. Yes, we are,' Mandy replied with a smile. She liked Walter, even though it seemed he could never remember her name. He was a cat lover with three cats of his own. One of them, Tom, was the fiercest, toughest cat in the village.

'I saw your grandad last night,' said Walter, looking at Mandy. 'Happened to mention my young grandson was going to Eileen Davy's for a violin lesson this morning and he told me you and the young sir would be there, too.'

'I'll say hello to Tommy for you if we see him,' promised Mandy.

'Though I expect we'll be more likely to hear him,' she added to James, once they were out of Walter's earshot.

'I'm glad *we're* not going for a violin lesson,' said James with a grin. 'I think I'd prefer to pick elderflowers.'

When they reached the Old School House a few minutes later, Eileen Davy bustled down the front path to meet them, her silver-blue hair looking immaculate as always. Mandy often thought not a single hair on Miss Davy's head would ever *dare* to move out of place!

'Good morning, Mandy. Good morning,

James,' said Miss Davy. They both immediately felt as though they were in the classroom at school.

'Good morning, Miss Davy,' they chorused.

'I do believe, James,' observed Miss Davy, 'that you're nearly as tall as Mandy now.' James blushed and pushed his glasses further up his nose. Mandy shot him a sympathetic look; she knew remarks like that embarrassed him.

'Shall we go straight round to the back garden, Miss Davy?' she asked brightly. 'We've got a pair of scissors each. And we've brought carrier bags to put the elderflowers in,' she added.

'I can see you have, Mandy,' said Miss Davy. 'And yes, do go round to the back garden. You'll have to get the small stepladders from the shed. I'm waiting for Tommy Pickard. He's a few minutes late for his lesson already.'

Mandy and James hurried off thankfully, then grinned at each other as Miss Davy called shrilly after them, 'And mind the hens!'

Miss Davy's hens were free-range hens. They wandered freely and happily all over the large back garden. As soon as they saw Mandy and James, they cackled their way eagerly towards them.

Mandy reached into a nearby feed-hopper, brought out a handful of grain and scattered it on the ground. 'There,' she chuckled, 'we'll leave them to squabble over it, while we fetch the stepladders.'

The Old School House garden backed on to a small forest and the elder trees lined the high, dry-stone wall that formed the boundary. Before long, Mandy and James were busily snipping the large clusters of creamy-white, sweet-scented blossoms.

Although they were right at the end of the garden, Tommy's efforts on the violin could be heard all too clearly. 'We'll be having Tommy's hamsters at Animal Ark with earache if he has to practise playing his violin at home,' said Mandy after a while.

'It can't go on for much longer, surely?' groaned James. 'He's been at it well over an hour. Even the woodpigeons are flying off in disgust,' he went on, as a loud clattering of wings added to the mournful sound of Tommy's violin.

'I thought I heard something else just then,' said Mandy, frowning slightly. 'But whatever it was, it's stopped.'

A few minutes later, the violin-playing stopped

too. 'Peace, perfect peace!' said James. 'All we need now is an ice-cold drink. This is really thirsty work.'

'I know. I keep thinking of the elderflower lemonade Gran's going to make.' Mandy sighed, tucking her hair behind her ears.

James took his glasses off and wiped his face. Then he asked hopefully, 'Can you see what I see, or am I hallucinating?'

Mandy peered between a couple of blossom-laden branches and smiled. Miss Davy was walking down the garden carrying a tray. On the tray were two tall glasses and, as Miss Davy got closer, Mandy could hear clinking ice.

'Come on down for refreshments!' Eileen Davy called.

James and Mandy didn't need to be asked twice. They came down their stepladders very quickly!

'Wow! Chocolate biscuits as well,' said James. 'Thank you, Miss Davy.'

'You've certainly been working hard, the pair of you,' Miss Davy praised, looking at the half-dozen or so overflowing carrier bags propped against a tree-trunk.

'Now,' she said briskly, 'you'd better eat your

biscuits before the squirrels pop over the wall and help themselves to them. They always seem to know when there's food around.'

Mandy was just reaching out towards the plate when she heard a faint 'maa-aaa' sound coming from somewhere in the forest.

'Did you hear that?' she said to James. 'That's the same noise I heard earlier. Listen, there it is again!'

A frown appeared on Miss Davy's forehead and she shook her head. 'I don't know what's making the noise,' she said, 'but I've heard it several times over the last two nights.'

'Maa-aaa-aaa.' It sounded pitiful this time and Mandy's heart lurched.

'It's an animal in trouble,' she cried. 'I know it is. Come on, James, we've got to find it!' Even as she was speaking, Mandy was moving one pair of stepladders towards the high wall.

'Do be careful, Mandy – it's a long way down!' Miss Davy warned.

'The ladder won't be tall enough!' said James as Mandy started climbing the rungs.

'We'll have to scramble the rest of the way up, then,' said Mandy, full of breathless determination. She stretched to her full height and managed to get her hands over the top of the wall. After that it was easy. She ended up with one leg either side of the wall.

Hauling James up wasn't so easy, but Miss Davy helped by mounting the steps behind him and pushing his feet as Mandy pulled his arms.

'Made it,' James puffed triumphantly and they sat on top of the wall for a moment as they got their breath back.

Another 'maa-aaa', fainter but somehow more desperate, rent the air and, without a second thought, Mandy made a wild leap for a strong-looking branch on a nearby tree. She slid herself down the trunk and looked around frantically.

'Maa-aaa-aaa.' There it was again. This time so faint it was impossible to tell which direction it was coming from.

'So *where* do we start looking?' asked James, landing with a rush next to Mandy.

'I think we'll have to wait and hope whatever it is makes the noise again,' Mandy said with a catch in her voice.

Two

The leafy trees cast dark shadows, making it hard for James and Mandy to see. But here and there the sun filtered through the foliage and their eyes soon adjusted.

Foxgloves stood high, twisting ivy claimed exposed tree roots, while tall bracken spread wide its uncurled fronds and everywhere, it seemed, large patches of shoulder-high, giant-sized nettles formed miniature forests of their own.

But smaller flowers had their way, too, and the scent from earthy-smelling chamomile hung heavily in the air.

Forest sounds were all around them; wood-pigeon, magpies and rooks calling, bees buzzing and small, secretive noises from the undergrowth. But the one sound Mandy and James were straining their ears to hear didn't come again.

Desperation and anguish mingled on Mandy's face as she looked at James. 'If only we knew what had made the noise we'd have some sort of clue where to look!'

'Well, it certainly wasn't a bird,' said James. 'And I don't think it was a squirrel, either, so . . .'

'Oh, I see what you're getting at. You mean whatever it is probably won't be up a tree but on the ground. Look at it, though, James,' Mandy gestured despairingly with her hands. 'Everywhere's so overgrown! And an injured or ill animal would hide itself really well for protection.'

James nodded. 'So we should look under a pile of old leaves or in the middle of a bush or a clump of nettles or bracken.'

'OK, so we'll split up and search every pile of leaves and look in the middle of every bush and every clump.' Mandy spoke decisively and glanced around again.

'We'll have to leave some sort of sign, stand a

stick in the ground or something like that, so we don't search the same place twice. Anything's better than standing here waiting.'

'We'll follow the narrow tracks, Mandy,' said James. 'It must have been animals who made them and they must lead somewhere!'

'Brilliant!' cried Mandy. 'You go to the left and I'll go to the right. We can search one side of each track first then when we get to the end, turn round and search the other side.'

'And leave twigs at both ends of the tracks to show where we've been.'

'If . . .' began Mandy, then she shook her head. 'No, *when* one of us finds it, we mustn't shout too loudly. We don't want to frighten it.'

'If we listen out for each other,' said James, 'we won't need to shout too loudly.'

'Right,' agreed Mandy. Anxious to start, she darted off to the right and towards the first narrow track.

As she glanced back over her shoulder, she heard James mutter, 'It's a shame I left Blackie at home. He could have helped!'

Feeling a little happier now they were doing something, Mandy smiled to herself. James's black Labrador was adorable but he'd have been more of a hindrance than a help. Especially here, where every other tree was a horse chestnut. To Blackie's mind, conker cases were baby hedgehogs and baby hedgehogs were something to yap and whine about!

Unfortunately, conkers, conker cases, acorns and old beech mast were about the only things Mandy *could* find! She made her way despondently up yet another narrow track, leaving it every now and then to peer into the centre of a bush or search through a pile of old leaves. And James obviously wasn't doing any better.

Mandy hadn't caught sight of him since they'd split up, but she knew she'd have heard him if he'd called. The woodpigeon and the other birds were quiet now.

Everything's quiet, she thought, standing for a moment and rolling her head to ease her aching neck. It was then that she heard it: a quiet, forlorn 'aaa-aaa'.

Heart thumping, eyes darting, Mandy crept forward. To her right was the largest clump of stinging nettles yet. Were the tops of some of them moving slightly? They were; she was *sure* they were!

Regardless of the cruel leaves attacking her bare legs and arms, she pushed her way into the centre of the clump. What she saw stopped her in her tracks. Two animals were lying ahead of her on a bed of flattened nettles.

Fallow deer. A mother and her baby. And the mother, Mandy knew for sure, was dead. The fawn, though, was moving its head and nudging weakly at its mother's body in a fruitless search for warmth, comfort and food.

Mandy called for James. She shouted his name. Then she took a few cautious steps forward and went down on her knees next to the fawn.

'All right, little one; we'll soon sort everything out,' Mandy said soothingly. She stretched out her hand and began to stroke the fawn.

It didn't seem to mind. The fawn looked at Mandy with bewildered eyes and gave a soft 'maaa'.

'I know, you're cold and hungry,' Mandy soothed. 'I can't do anything about your hunger yet, but . . .' Mandy pulled off her cotton over-shirt.

'There,' she said, placing it over the fawn. 'And you can have James's shirt, too, when he finds us.' Mandy stood up and raised her hands to her mouth to call James again.

But there was no need; just then James came running into sight. 'What is it?' he panted as soon as he was close. 'What have you found, Mandy?'

'A fallow deer fawn. The mother's dead and the fawn's cold and hungry. Take your T-shirt off, James.'

James whipped it off then moved forward. 'Oh, Mandy,' he gulped, gently placing his shirt over the fawn, 'will we be able to save her?'

'Mum and Dad will,' replied Mandy, but she crossed her fingers as she spoke. The fawn looked very weak. 'And,' she continued, wiping a tear away, 'I'll get Dad to come back later, to bury the mother. She was such a pretty thing, James.' Mandy stood up and looked round.

'I think she must have been injured by a car,' said James. 'There's a gash on her head and another on her side. But she managed to make her way back to her baby,' he added, his voice shaking a little.

'Yes,' said Mandy, moving away towards some large trees. 'Now *we've* got to get the baby out of here.'

Mandy was looking around for some sturdy branches to make a stretcher with. James guessed what she was thinking and scrambled to his feet to help.

'Branches about this length should be OK,' said James, picking one up.

Mandy nodded. 'We'll have to use the belts from our shorts to hold the branches together,' she said.

'And our socks,' suggested James. 'We can take them off and tie them together.'

They worked swiftly; they knew it was essential to get the fawn to Animal Ark as quickly as possible. Before long, they were lifting the fawn on to the makeshift stretcher.

James had a better sense of direction than Mandy so he went in front, his arms stretched behind him to carry his end of the stretcher. But they were both wondering how they'd get themselves and the fawn back over Miss Davy's wall when they got there.

It seemed as though their journey was taking for ever. Their arms and legs were aching and covered in painful blotches from the stinging nettles.

At last, though, the wall was in sight. And to

Mandy and James's relief, Miss Davy was standing their side of the wall.

As they got close she said briskly, 'I phoned your father, Mandy, and told him you and James were searching for an animal. One which sounded like it needed attention.'

'It does,' said Mandy. 'It's a fawn, Miss Davy. The mother is dead and this poor little thing is starving. Is Dad coming? Is he on his way?'

'He'll be waiting on the road,' said Miss Davy, moving forward to help with the weight of the stretcher. 'There's a stile a short distance past the far boundary wall. It's easy enough to climb over, I came in that way. Come on, I'll guide you to it.'

Mandy smiled a little as Miss Davy efficiently took charge. 'To your left a little, James. Watch out for the holly tree . . . Mind the low branches of the wild laburnum . . . Don't get too close to the wall, the rabbits have been burrowing there.'

Then Mandy saw her dad striding towards them, carrying his vet's bag, and her smile widened.

'I felt so helpless just waiting,' said Adam Hope, 'but I didn't dare wander round too much in case I missed you. Now, what have you found this time?' But even as he was speaking, he'd put his bag down and his hands were already moving over the fawn.

'She's badly dehydrated,' he said, 'and starving. I don't think there's any actual injury, though. Was there any sign of the mother, Mandy?'

'Dead,' Mandy said sadly. 'Will you . . . ?'

'Don't worry, we'll sort that out later, I promise.' Adam Hope reassured Mandy that the mother deer would be buried.

'Now though, I think it will be quicker . . .' he suited action to words and lifted the fawn, '. . . if I carry the fawn from here. You can bring my bag, Mandy.'

'Go on, you two,' Miss Davy said to Mandy and James. 'Leave the stretcher with me, I'll make my own way back. And I'll phone Animal Ark to let them know you're on your way.'

'Thank you, Miss Davy,' said Mandy, and she and James hurried to catch up with her dad.

'Did we find her in time, Mr Hope?' asked James. 'Will she live?'

'She's got a reasonable chance, I think. She isn't a newborn, I'd say she's about a month or so old. But she needs some fluid intake quickly.

And she'll need feeding every three hours or so for the next few days.'

'No problem,' said James. 'Mandy and I will be able to help a lot. We're off school next week for half-term.'

They reached the stile and Mandy said, 'James and I will hold her, then pass her to you when you're over, Dad.'

The fawn's eyes were closed and she lay in their arms without stirring. 'Don't you give up now, Sprite,' Mandy whispered. 'Not now we've got you safely this far.'

'Sprite?' queried James, as Mr Hope took the fawn and strode towards the Animal Ark Land-rover.

'I know!' Mandy replied defensively as she climbed wearily over the stile. 'She's a wild animal, not a pet, so I shouldn't give her a name. But . . .'

'It's a good name, Mandy,' James said, as he followed her over. 'She is a sprite, a little wood sprite.'

Mandy turned her head and smiled her thanks for his support. Blushing slightly, James returned the smile, then they both darted down the bank to the Land-rover.

Mr Hope had already placed Sprite in the back on a fleecy blanket and was gently squeezing the lower part of her tummy.

'If she hasn't been drinking or feeding for a couple of days, it's unlikely she's emptied her bladder,' he explained. 'I want to make her do that before getting some fluid into her.'

'It's worked, Dad,' said Mandy. 'Look.' Sprite had made a small puddle on the blanket.

'What will you give her now, Mr Hope?' asked James. 'Glucose water?'

'No, she needs something more than that. I'll have to put her on an intravenous drip. And I don't think we'll chance waiting until we get back to Animal Ark, either.'

Mandy had her dad's vet bag open almost before he'd finished speaking. 'What do you want out, Dad?'

'Hartmanns, please, love,' he replied. 'It's a liquid to correct fluid balance,' he explained to James. 'It's got minerals in as well.'

'You'll have to hold the bag up, Mandy, then the solution will drip down through this tube . . .' Mr Hope pointed to it and Mandy nodded, '. . . and through the needle which I'll put into a vein in Sprite's front leg.'

'I'll get in and kneel up behind Sprite, ready to hold the bag up, Dad,' said Mandy.

'You make a good assistant,' he said, and Mandy looked delighted. Being a good assistant would do for now. She'd decided long ago that she wanted to train to be a vet when she left school.

Mr Hope worked swiftly. Before long he said, 'Right, you hop in the front, James, and we'll be off.'

Once they were moving, nobody spoke for a while. Mandy stroked the fawn gently and hoped her parents would agree to keeping it at Animal Ark until it was strong enough to be released back into the forest.

James turned round, caught Mandy's eye and gave a small smile. He seemed to know exactly what she was thinking!

'All right, Mandy? Not long now,' said Mr Hope.

'Her eyes are closed but I don't think she's really asleep,' Mandy replied.

'It's a good job Sprite can't see *that*!' chuckled James, as they drove along the High Street. 'It really would frighten her. Look, Mandy, Mrs Ponsonby's got a new hat!'

Mrs Ponsonby lived in Bleakfell Hall, off one of the narrow moorland roads above the village. She thought of herself as 'the Lady of the Manor' and dressed and acted accordingly. Today she was wearing a blue dress patterned with pink and white roses and a white cartwheel-shaped hat with bunches of pansies all over it.

'Carrying Pandora again, too,' observed Adam Hope, shaking his head. 'She brought that Pekinese to Animal Ark this morning. No matter how many times I tell her the dog needs more exercise, she just refuses to listen.'

'Oh, yes, you're meant to be on surgery duty, aren't you, Dad?' Mandy recalled.

'I was, but your mum took over after Miss Davy phoned,' he replied. 'She had to stay in because she's expecting Ernie Bell round to measure up for some new kitchen cupboards.'

'Don't remind me,' groaned Mandy. 'I promised I'd empty the old cupboards out during half-term.'

By now, they'd turned into the lane that led to Animal Ark. Two minutes later they arrived and Emily Hope was hurrying round the corner of the house from the surgery to meet them.

James got out and joined her at the back of the vehicle as she was opening it.

'You got here quicker than I thought you would,' she said.

'It felt like a long time to me, Mrs Hope,' James replied.

'I second that,' said Mandy. 'But I think Sprite is feeling a little bit better now,' she added, giving her mum a smile.

Emily Hope smiled reassuringly back at her, then said, 'I think I'd feel better if you and James were to go straight indoors to get the first-aid box and put some cream on your nettle stings. No arguments,' she added firmly, as she gently lifted the fawn out.

'Yes, leave her to us now, love,' Mr Hope said with a sympathetic smile.

'And get yourselves something to eat and drink after you've seen to those stings,' ordered Emily Hope. 'There's salad and home-made veggie burgers in the fridge,' she called as she and Mr Hope disappeared round the corner of the house with the fawn.

'I can't wait any longer to see how Sprite's getting on,' said Mandy after they had eaten.

'Come on, James, let's go through and find out.'

They found Adam and Emily Hope in the annexe, the little room at the back of the residential unit. It was set up especially for wild animals that needed treatment. They had to be kept separate from the other patients to avoid cross-infection.

'How is she?' Mandy asked anxiously, kneeling down to look in the cage.

Her mum's green eyes were concerned. 'She's very weak from lack of nourishment. What she really needs is milk.'

'I don't understand the problem,' said Mandy. 'I know we mustn't handle her too much in case she starts to think one of us is her mother, but surely that doesn't mean we can't feed her milk from a bottle?'

'Of course it doesn't, love.' It was Mandy's dad who replied.

'The problem is that she's too weak to stand,' Mrs Hope explained gently. 'And fawns need to be standing up to feed.'

'Maybe she's just too tired to bother,' said James. 'If she has a sleep she might take some milk when she wakes up.'

'Yes, that's what we're hoping,' Mrs Hope

agreed, but Mandy could tell her mum wasn't too happy about things.

'Look at her, though,' Mandy said brokenly. 'She isn't asleep. She's lying with her eyes open. With a sort of faraway look.'

'Well, she is in strange surroundings,' Mr Hope pointed out. 'She's used to the forest and forest noises.'

'That's it, Dad!' Mandy jumped to her feet and hugged him. Then she turned to James, 'Come on, we've got work to do!'

'OK,' said James. He didn't bother to ask where they were going or what they'd be doing. He knew Mandy had an idea to help Sprite. That was good enough for him.

'We'll be back in a little while,' Mandy told her parents, as she and James hurried out through the annexe door.

Three

'I'll get my bike, James. You go to the old shed.'

'What am I supposed to be getting?' called James.

'Two pairs of gardening gloves,' Mandy called back over her shoulder. 'They'll be in the top drawer of the sideboard at the back of the shed. And bring a couple of strong poly bags as well.'

Mandy had been dashing towards the garage as she spoke but suddenly, she retraced her steps and made for the washing hanging on the line.

'Dad's fleecy-lined lumber-shirts,' she gloated, unpegging one for herself and one for James. 'Mum must have washed them to give Gran for the WI's "good-as-new" stall. I'll just have to wash them again if we mess them up.'

'She's like a whirlwind when she gets going,' James muttered to himself, watching Mandy race towards the garage again.

'We'll take the short cut down the back lane,' Mandy announced, arriving by the shed with her own and James's bike. She gave him one of the shirts and took one of the polythene bags.

'Short cut to where?' asked James. He followed Mandy's example and put the shirt into the bag and tied the bag round the handlebars of his bike. Then he shoved his glasses more securely up on his nose.

'Short cut to where?' he repeated as he climbed on to his bike.

'Ernie Bell's. For nettles from his wild patch,' Mandy said with a grin. 'That's what the gloves, shirts and poly bags are for. We could go to Monkton Spinney,' she added, 'but seeing as Ernie lives near Walter Pickard it'll be better if we go there.' Mandy had that determined look on her face again as she gave a quick sideways glance at James.

'OK, I give in,' he said obligingly. 'What's Walter got to do with any of this?'

'You know how Dad said Sprite was used to the forest and forest noises?' said Mandy.

'Which is why we're going to get some nettles,' said James. 'So we can put them in her cage for her to lie on.'

'We're going to wind them through the mesh of the cage door, too,' said Mandy. 'You know, sort of camouflage it.'

'You still haven't told me where Walter comes into it, though,' James pointed out.

'Listen, James, do you remember Walter playing us that tape a few weeks ago? *Sounds of Nature*, I think it was called. There were animal noises, leaves rustling in the breeze, and lots of different birdcalls.'

'Mandy, that's a great idea!' James swerved and just managed to avoid knocking Mandy off her bike. 'If he'll let us borrow the tape and his cassette player . . .'

Mandy laughed and pedalled even faster. 'We can bring the *sounds* of the forest to the annexe as well and Sprite will really feel at home!'

An hour later, Mandy and James returned to Animal Ark with two polythene bags full of large nettle plants, Walter's tape, his cassette player and a spare pack of batteries.

Adam and Emily Hope were sitting in the garden and Mandy quickly explained her idea.

'It might help if she has something familiar around her,' her dad agreed. 'She did get to her feet for a while but she rejected the milk.'

'It certainly won't do any harm,' said her mum. 'Not to the fawn, anyway.'

'Nor to us, Mum,' Mandy opened up one of the bags and pulled out her dad's fleecy-lined lumber-shirts and the two pairs of gardening gloves. 'I borrowed these,' she said. 'We wore them while we were pulling up the plants in Ernie's wild patch.' She passed a shirt and a pair of gloves to James. 'We'll wear them again now. I promise I'll wash them again when James and I have finished with them,' Mandy went on quickly.

'I'm glad to hear it. They're for Gran's stall,' said Emily Hope, but she was smiling as she spoke. 'And speaking of Gran . . .'

'Cripes!' said James. 'We forgot all about your gran's elderflowers, Mandy. And we'd picked loads of them, too.'

'I'll pop round and explain after we've made Sprite feel more at home,' said Mandy.

'If you two will just let me finish, I'm trying to tell you that Eileen Davy phoned to say she'd already taken the elderflowers round to Gran's,' said Mrs Hope. 'And she's told Gran about the fawn.'

'That's good,' said Mandy. 'I'd still like to go round, though, to tell Gran and Grandad *all* about Sprite. Come on, James, let's go in and arrange these nettles.'

'I'll come in, too,' said Mrs Hope, getting up from her lounger. 'I want to check on the blood-hound.'

'Oh, Mum!' gasped Mandy. 'I forgot about poor Humphrey. Has he had his operation? Did you remove the cysts? Is he OK?'

'Yes to all three questions,' replied her mum. 'It was only a short job. He should be coming round by now.'

'And I want to restock my emergency pack,' said Adam Hope, following them in. 'Though I'm hoping for a nice quiet weekend with no more call-outs.'

'Oh, one thing, Dad,' said Mandy, delving into one of the bags. 'Walter Pickard gave us this scratching-post. He got it for his cats but never got round to putting it up. It's still in its box, look. He thought we could put it in the cage for Sprite to rub against. Is that OK?'

'Yes, but just give it a wipe over with very weak disinfectant first,' Mr Hope advised, then smiled after them as they hurried through to the annexe.

Sprite seemed to be sleeping. Mandy opened the door quietly and began to carefully pile a few nettle plants around her.

James set the cassette player going and smiled at the cooing of woodpigeons. 'That should make Sprite feel more at home,' he said.

'I think it already is,' Mandy said quietly.

'Look, James! She's opened her eyes. She's sniffing at the nettles.'

They watched her for a minute or two. The
little fawn certainly seemed to be taking more
interest in her surroundings now.

'I'll thread the rest of the nettles through the
mesh on the door if you'll wipe the scratching-
post down, James,' suggested Mandy. 'Then we'll
leave her for a while before trying her with some
milk again.'

When they'd finished in the annexe they
scrubbed their hands and went through to see
Humphrey. He gazed at them sleepily with his
sorrowful eyes, but he wagged his tail when
Mandy spoke to him.

'He's doing fine,' Emily Hope said cheerfully.
'What are you two going to do now?'

'Feed the rabbits,' replied Mandy. 'Then I'm
going to Gran and Grandad's and James is going
home to take Blackie for a walk.'

'I'll come back later to see Sprite if that's OK,
Mrs Hope,' said James.

'Of course it is, James. We thought we'd have
a barbecue later this evening once it's gone a bit
cooler. Ask your parents if you can stay and tell
them one of us will run you home afterwards.'

'That'd be great,' said James. 'Thanks, Mrs Hope.'

Together, Mandy and James fed the rabbits and gave them some fresh water. Mandy told them she'd put them out in their run later. 'It's too hot for you to lollop around just yet,' she said.

'I think they know it's too hot for them to run around,' said James. 'They usually scrabble at the cage door, asking to come out, but they're not doing it today. Ernie's squirrel was exactly the same, too hot to be bothered.'

'You're right, Sammy wasn't his usual chatty self,' agreed Mandy. 'I expect it takes animals longer than us to get used to day after day of sunshine. I heard on the radio that, so far, it's been one of the hottest Junes on record!'

Mandy decided she would walk to her grand-parents' cottage. So James went home on his bike and Mandy set off on foot, up the lane to Lilac Cottage.

As was often the case, Mandy's grandad was in his greenhouse. But what was unusual, Mandy noticed as she approached, was that Grandad wasn't actually *doing* anything. He was just standing, staring into space, with a frown on his face.

The frown lifted slightly when he saw Mandy, and he came out to greet her. 'Hello, Mandy my love. How's the fawn? Let's go into the kitchen and see Gran; she's busy snipping elder-flowers for the lemonade.'

Mandy linked her hand through his arm and they started walking up the garden. 'Oh, look at Smoky,' she laughed, pointing to her grand-parents' mischievous little cat. He was in one of Grandad's flowerbeds, standing on his hind legs in an effort to catch a dragonfly zooming round and round above the tall lupins.

Grandad glanced in the direction Mandy was pointing and nodded his head. But he didn't make any comment, which wasn't like him at all!

'Is anything the matter, Grandad?' asked Mandy. 'You don't seem yourself. Are you all right?'

'No, he isn't!' said Gran. She'd heard Mandy's voice through the open back door and had come outside.

Mandy ran to give her a hug then Gran went on, 'He's hopping mad, Mandy, and I don't blame him!'

Mandy looked from one to the other in amazement. She'd seen Gran get mad about things, 'up on her high horse' they called it. But not Grandad. It was a family joke that nothing could make Grandad lose his temper.

'Why?' demanded Mandy. 'What's happened?'

'Someone . . .' spluttered Grandad, '. . . someone has stolen the Bedfordshire Champion!'

Mandy racked her brains, trying to think which of the local farmers had an animal who'd won that title. 'Who does it belong to?' she asked at last. 'And have they reported it? Mum and Dad usually get to hear about anything like that, so they can keep a look out. But they haven't said anything.'

'How could your mum or dad keep a look out?' Grandad said irritably. 'Much as I love the two of them, they don't know one onion from another.'

'Onions!' Mandy spluttered with amusement. 'I'm sorry, Grandad,' she said, when she saw the look on his face. 'I thought the Bedfordshire Champion was a bull or a ram.'

Grandad's eyes twinkled and his lips twitched in amusement.

'Oh, Mandy love,' he chuckled, 'that's the first

laugh I've had all day. Mind,' he added quickly, looking stern again, 'it doesn't take away from the fact that someone has stolen all the best onions from Harry Morton's allotment while I'm supposed to be looking after it for him! Vandals, that's what they are. Vandals!'

'Why should anyone steal them?' asked Mandy. 'I mean, they might be special to Harry Morton and you, Grandad, but nobody would get much money for them if they tried to sell them. Besides,' she said, shaking her head, 'none of the kids in Welford would steal from the allotments. I'm sure they wouldn't.'

Grandad snorted angrily. 'It wasn't the work of kids, Mandy! No, it was an adult. And they haven't been stolen to be sold. Oh, no! The Bedfordshire Champions have been stolen to prevent Harry and me from winning a prize at the Vegetable Show next month! I'd lifted them and laid them out to dry; anyone with half a mind would've been able to see they were prize-winners.'

'But who'd do something like that?' gasped Mandy.

'I don't know for sure,' Grandad replied grimly. 'A similar thing happened a few years back. It was gooseberries that disappeared then. We never did find out who took them.'

Grandad pursed his lips and nodded his head, then went on, 'But this time a few allotment holders and I intend to find out. The allotments will be guarded day and night from now on. We've got a rota up. I'm on guard tonight from midnight 'til six in the morning.'

Mandy bit her lip. She didn't like to think of her grandad spending all night alone, guarding the allotments. It could be really dangerous if the thief turned up! She glanced at her gran, eyebrows raised in question. Surely Gran wouldn't be happy about it, either?

But to Mandy's surprise Gran nodded her head in agreement. 'I'm going with him,' she said. 'We're going to park the camper van as close to the allotments as we can and keep a watch in comfort.'

'But – ' Mandy began in protest.

'It's all settled, Mandy,' said Gran. 'But that's enough of our problems. Come into the kitchen. You can help me finish off the elderflowers while you tell us how you and James found the fawn.'

'And how it's getting on now,' added Grandad.

'I'll have to tell you quickly,' said Mandy. 'I want to get back and see if I can persuade her to take some milk.'

So Mandy sat down at the table with a pair of kitchen scissors and Gran told her how to carefully remove the elderflowers from the stems.

'Then we wash them and put them in earthenware containers with lemon juice and rind, sugar, vinegar and water,' Gran explained. 'We leave them for forty-eight hours then strain the liquid off into screwtop bottles. The lemonade will be ready in two weeks, just in time for the Fete.'

'Dorothy,' scolded Grandad, 'we're supposed to be hearing about the fawn. Let the lass tell us!'

Mandy told them about Sprite in double-quick time. Just talking about the poor fawn made Mandy want to get back to Animal Ark. She said she'd have to go.

'Take some of my fresh-baked gingerbread with you, Mandy,' said Gran. 'You can have it for tea.'

'I don't think we'll be having tea today,' Mandy told her. 'We'll be saving ourselves for the barbecue we're having later. I'll try and save the gingerbread for then, too. I don't know if I'll manage, though. It looks delicious.'

'I'll cut you off a slice to eat on your way home,' said Gran, her eyes twinkling.

'We'll take a good slab with us tonight,' said Grandad. 'We might as well enjoy ourselves while we're waiting to catch that vandal.'

Those words spurred Mandy on. She kissed her grandparents goodbye and hurried all the way home.

Four

As Mandy arrived at Animal Ark, Humphrey's owner was just driving away. Mandy waved and went round the corner of the house to the surgery.

'Geoff's been to collect the jird as well, so, with any luck, it looks as if we'll only have Sprite to worry about for the rest of the weekend,' said Adam Hope.

'That's what you think,' Mandy told him.

'Don't tell me you've found another wild animal needing attention?' Her dad gave his lop-sided smile and pointed to the small package Mandy was carrying.

Mandy grinned. 'Gingerbread from Gran,' she said. Then her smile faded and she spoke more seriously. 'It isn't another animal we need to worry about. It's Gran and Grandad . . .'

'I'll go round right away,' said Adam Hope when Mandy had finished telling him the tale about the thief at the allotments. 'Though I doubt I'll be able to talk them out of guard duty. Not when they're *both* set on it.'

'I'll go through and look at Sprite,' said Mandy.

'Have a word with your mum first,' Mr Hope told her. 'Tell her I'll be back soon.'

Mandy looked thoughtfully after her dad as he disappeared. He'd seemed almost glad to be going out. *Which means Mum's going to say something I won't like hearing*, thought Mandy. *And I think I can guess what that will be.*

She went slowly through the connecting door between the surgery and the house and wandered into the kitchen, where Emily Hope was preparing the food for the barbecue.

'Gran sent some gingerbread,' said Mandy, putting the package down on the table. 'And Dad's gone round there just now to . . .' Mandy's voice trailed off.

Mrs Hope stopped what she was doing and looked at Mandy.

'All right,' said Mandy. 'I know what you're going to say. I know we can't keep Sprite here once she's better. But she isn't better yet and . . .'

'That's just it, Mandy. 'I'm not sure she will get better. Unless there's something obvious, it's very hard to diagnose wild animals. We don't know enough because wild animals aren't part of our everyday life. And I'm wondering if the fawn was already ill before the mother doe died from her injuries.'

'What makes you think that, Mum?' Mandy asked worriedly.

'Well, Dad and I reckon Sprite is about four weeks old. Fawns are usually very active at that age and able to lap water and maybe even graze a little. But Sprite obviously hasn't had any fluid for at least a couple of days.'

'But everywhere is so dry, Mum. Maybe she couldn't find any water to lap.'

'That's a possibility. And of course we'll do our very best for her. I'd feel happier if she'd show a bit of interest in milk when it's offered. True, it sometimes takes quite a while for an orphan to accept milk from a bottle, but Sprite didn't even lick her lips when I rubbed her mouth with a milky finger.'

'Maybe she's still too scared to trust us yet,' said Mandy.

'Again, it's a possibility. But don't build your hopes up too high, Mandy, that's all. And if she does recover . . .'

'*When* Sprite recovers,' Mandy said determinedly, 'James and I will think of something. And now I'll go and see if she'll stand up and take some milk. Did you try her on Vita-milk or carton milk, Mum?'

'Diluted carton milk,' replied Emily Hope. 'She's getting plenty of vitamins and other supplements from the Hartmanns.'

'Would Vita-milk be OK, though? She might like the taste of that more.'

'She might,' Mrs Hope agreed. 'Add more water than usual to it, Mandy, and give it a try. And wear the surgery coat I was wearing when I tried to feed her. I've left it in the annexe. It might help if we wear the same thing every time so Sprite gets used to the smell of it.'

As Mandy went back through the connecting door into the surgery, she kept her hopes up by thinking of some of the wild animals they'd successfully helped in the past.

Ernie Bell's squirrel, Humbug the badger cub, a newborn fox cub, a hedgehog with a broken leg, a baby owl . . .

'And now there's Sprite,' she murmured, as she reached for her mum's green surgery coat. 'She'll be a success story, too!'

Mandy undid a packet of vitamin-milk powder, sprinkled some into a feeding bottle, added some boiled water and shook the bottle to mix the mixture up.

Then she rewound the tape and started it playing again before moving to Sprite's cage with the feeding bottle. She kneeled down and opened the door then leaned back on her heels and kept as still as possible.

Sprite was lying on the nettle plants, curled up like a sleeping cat. But she wasn't asleep. For a few minutes, she gazed unblinkingly at Mandy with soft, round eyes and Mandy had to swallow hard; Sprite had such a pretty face. Her nose looked like dark velvet and the fur between her softly pointed ears looked velvety, too. Her coat was reddish-yellow with dozens and dozens of pure white spots which started at the back of her neck.

There was a slight movement then . . . Mandy held her breath as the fawn rose unsteadily to her feet. Her legs were long, like a foal's, and her underparts a delicate primrose-white. Sprite moved her head from side to side then she lowered it, putting her nose close to the drip feed in her front leg.

Don't pull the needle out of the vein, Sprite, Mandy prayed silently. Her prayer was answered. Sprite lifted her head, took a nervous half-step towards the open cage door, then stopped.

Moving as slowly as she could, Mandy reached towards Sprite's mouth with the feeding bottle. Sprite stepped back, but she stayed on her feet. Mandy reached a bit closer and this time managed to rub the teat around Sprite's mouth.

Sprite stayed as still as a statue and Mandy, her tongue moving over her own lips as if to encourage the little fawn, continued her movement with the feeding bottle.

Then Sprite jerked her head away and sank back down on to the nettles.

Fighting back tears of disappointment, Mandy slowly drew her arm out and quietly closed the cage door. She got up and saw her dad standing in the doorway. 'That's the best attempt yet,' he said softly. 'And, you know, Mandy, the drip is probably unsettling her as much as anything. You might be more successful when we take it away tomorrow.'

Mandy smiled and nodded, before pouring the Vita-milk mixture into a screwtop bottle and putting it in the little fridge they used for the animals' food.

'The teat didn't go in her mouth,' she said, 'but I'll put it and the feeding bottle in the steriliser to be on the safe side. Then we'll go and find Mum and you can tell us what happened when you went to Gran and Grandad's.'

Back inside Emily Hope had poured three glasses of iced lemonade. Mandy quickly gave her a progress report on Sprite, then they all sat down at the kitchen table to hear about Adam Hope's visit to his parents.

'I couldn't talk them out of it,' he said. 'Stubborn as mules, the pair of them. But I managed to persuade them to take a mobile phone with them. I lent them our spare one, and they promised they'd phone for help if anyone suspicious turns up.'

'Did they promise they'd wait for help to arrive, though?' demanded Mandy.

'More or less,' Adam Hope replied with a wry grin. He mimicked Gran's tone perfectly: 'As long as waiting for help doesn't mean the culprit getting away.'

Just then, James arrived. Mrs Hope poured him a glass of lemonade and Mandy brought him up to date.

'Maybe I should lend your gran and grandad Blackie,' he said.

'Oh, James,' laughed Mandy. 'Blackie would probably welcome the thief like a long-lost friend.'

James grinned and said, 'You're right.' Blackie was far too friendly ever to be a watch dog.

'I don't suppose the police would help?' said Mandy.

'As it happens,' said Mr Hope, 'I did see PC Burton on my way home. He promised he'd ask the night patrol car to pass that way at regular intervals. We can't do any more than that. Now if we're going to eat tonight, I'd better get the barbecue lit.'

'James and I will let the rabbits have a bit of a run around, then come back and help,' said Mandy.

While they were playing with the rabbits,

Mandy told James what her mum had said about Sprite.

'Don't worry, Mandy. Your parents are terrific vets; they'll get her right, you'll see.'

Mandy flashed him a grateful smile and he immediately became very busy stroking Mopsy.

'I'm sure you want to see Sprite again,' said Mandy ignoring his embarrassment, 'but we mustn't disturb her more than necessary.'

'That's OK,' James said, 'I'll be seeing a lot of her when she starts feeding from the bottle. I won't be able to help much tomorrow.' He pulled a face. 'We've got relations coming for Sunday lunch and tea. After that, though, I'll take my turn.'

Twenty-four hours later, Sprite was still refusing to take any milk. 'She does seem to be brighter, though,' said James. 'She reminds me of a new-born foal trying to take its first steps,' he added softly as Sprite backed away a bit. 'And look at her eyes, Mandy; they've lost that helpless, frightened look.'

James had come round as soon as his visitors had left and arrived just in time to see Mandy trying once more to feed the little fawn.

'Yes, the Hartmanns did its job. Sprite has been moving round more since Dad took the drip out,' Mandy replied quietly. 'That was a good few hours ago.'

'I see you've put fresh nettles everywhere,' said James.

'I got them from Ernie's wild patch again,' said Mandy. 'I left some of yesterday's nettles inside the cage, so Sprite could still smell her own scent. Then I stayed with her for ages after I'd cleaned the cage out, talking to her and letting her smell my hand. She's come to trust me, I know she has.'

Mandy shook her head and went on, 'But she should be more than ready for some milk by now. I'm sure she isn't refusing to feed because she's frightened.'

'Maybe you wanting so much for her to feed is making you a bit tense,' suggested James. 'Maybe it's putting her off.'

'You could be right,' agreed Mandy.

'Tell you what,' said James. 'It would do you good to have a break. I've left Blackie in the garden with your dad. Let's take him for a walk by the river. We can feed the ducks and we might see the swans with their cygnets.'

'Good idea,' said Mandy, closing the cage door and getting stiffly to her feet. 'We can call in on Gran and Grandad as well. Dad's spoken to them today but I haven't.'

'I'd forgotten about their night-watch,' said James. 'Did anything happen?'

Mandy chuckled, 'Nothing apart from Gran almost hitting a policeman with her umbrella. Apparently he parked behind them and went and knocked on the camper van window to let them know he was there.'

'And not knowing who it was, your gran got ready for battle,' laughed James. 'Gosh, I'd like to have seen her face when she realised her mistake!'

Mandy emptied the feeding bottle before popping it into the steriliser. Then she and James went out into the garden.

'Any luck?' Adam Hope asked.

Mandy shook her head gloomily and bent to fondle Blackie, who'd bounded forward to greet her. 'We're going to take Blackie for a walk by the river, then call in at Lilac Cottage. I'll try again when I come home,' she said.

'Put some anti-midge lotion on if you're going by the river,' advised her dad. 'They'll be out in their millions on an evening like this.'

'OK,' said Mandy, straightening up and turning to face her dad. 'Dad, how long can Sprite go without milk, before . . . ?' Mandy gulped, then bit her lip, unable to finish the question.

Mandy's parents were always honest with her. They never gave her false hopes. After all, as much as they tried to, they couldn't cure every single animal who came to them.

Now, Adam Hope stroked his beard thoughtfully as Mandy and James, their eyes large and anxious, waited for his reply.

'I really don't know how long Sprite can go without milk,' Mr Hope replied slowly. 'But I think if she hasn't taken any by this time tomorrow . . . Well, the odds will be stacked pretty heavily against her. And then—' he broke off and looked meaningfully at Mandy.

Mandy stared back at her dad for a long moment then said in a muffled voice, 'You wait here a minute, James. I'll go and get the lotion and some bread for the ducks.'

James nodded. He knew Mandy needed to be alone for a while.

Five

Adam Hope watched his daughter go inside. He turned to James and said, 'Feeling helpless, not knowing the answers, is one of the hardest things about being a vet.'

'You know the answers *most* of the time!' protested James.

'Mmm, luckily, it isn't too often that we don't. But we don't know why Sprite won't take any milk. Mandy's mum and I have both had a good look at her and we can't see any obvious reason. Her mouth, her tongue and throat seem to be all right.'

'Do you think there could be something

wrong with her stomach?' asked James.

'There could be,' said Mr Hope.

James stared thoughtfully over the garden then blurted out, 'You said the odds would be stacked against Sprite if she hasn't started to feed by this time tomorrow. Does that mean you'd have to put her to sleep?'

'Sometimes,' Mr Hope said gently, 'hard decisions have to be taken.'

'You mean like when Benji developed that growth on his brain and had to be put to sleep,' James said sadly. 'I still miss that cat you know, even though we've got Eric now. But Benji would have been in pain.'

Mr Hope nodded and met James's gaze steadily.

'I see what you're getting at,' said James. 'Sprite might be in pain. That might be why she won't take any milk.'

'As far as I can tell, James, Sprite doesn't seem to be in pain. And we won't give up yet. But we can't do anything for her if she won't feed. Because, in the end, she would be in pain.' Then he shrugged, gave a half-smile and said, 'However, if patience, determination and perseverance is what it takes, Mandy and you are the ones to pull her through.'

James blushed with pleasure, but he was glad Mandy returned at that point and handed him the bottle of anti-midge lotion. 'This stuff smells terrible,' he said as he rubbed it on his neck and arms.

'Just hope the midges agree,' smiled Mr Hope, ruffling Mandy's hair and adding gently, 'All right, love?'

Mandy nodded and said, 'We'll see you later, Dad. We won't be too long.'

'Well, enjoy your walk, both of you.' Blackie barked loudly and Mr Hope added with a laugh, 'You too, of course, Blackie.'

Mandy and James didn't speak as they walked down the driveway and out on to the lane. They were both thinking about Sprite and what Mr Hope had said.

But, after a while James said stoutly, 'Twenty-four hours is a long time, Mandy. If someone tries to feed Sprite every three hours, that's eight goes. She'll be gulping milk down like a greedy lamb before then, you'll see.'

Mandy nodded. 'You could be right. But maybe I shouldn't have come out, James. 'It might have been better staying with Sprite. Maybe I didn't try hard enough to get her to suck the teat. I should have spoken really firmly to her instead of trying to coax her. Maybe I should have even held her mouth open and shoved the bottle in. I could have got Mum or Dad to hold her from behind so she couldn't lie down.'

'This walk was a good idea,' James replied. 'Sometimes you can think more clearly about a problem if you're away from it for a while. But I think you're being a bit hard on yourself. I'm sure you've done everything right. And Sprite *has* started to trust you. That means you'll be able to treat her more firmly next time you try her with the bottle.'

Mandy was surprised by James's little speech. True, he always supported her, backed her up in things, but he didn't usually put it into words. He was usually too shy or embarrassed to do that.

Then, as if to prove her thoughts right, James abruptly changed the subject by saying, 'And now . . . race you to the end of the lane!'

'It's too hot!' Mandy protested. But James was already off, with Blackie bounding enthusiastically at his heels. Mandy flew after them and they all reached the road together.

They stood there for a moment, catching their breath; then they heard the metallic chimes of an ice-cream van.

James lunged forward and grabbed Blackie. 'Gotcha!' he chuckled, clipping Blackie's lead on. The Labrador knew exactly what those chimes meant; ice-cream was one of his weaknesses.

'Blackie's got the right idea, though,' laughed Mandy. 'I wonder if we can make it to the village green before the ice-cream van goes?'

They did make it. There was quite a queue at the van; it stretched almost to the pond at the far end of the green. Blackie whined and pulled on his lead. He liked swimming in the pond.

'No, Blackie. You stand in the queue with us,' James said sternly.

'Now, then,' said Walter Pickard, waiting to buy a giant cone for Tommy, his grandson. 'And how's the latest waif and stray, young miss?'

Mandy tucked her hair behind her ears and said, 'She's not feeding yet. But,' she added determinedly, 'there's still time for that.'

'Aye,' Walter said wisely. 'Have to get a wild animal to trust you first. You stick at it, young miss.'

'Hello, Mandy. Hello, James,' said Tommy. 'I've been fishing in the pond. I didn't catch any fish but I caught four tadpoles! Look!' Tommy held up a jamjar and Mandy and James admired the tadpoles.

Then Tommy looked at Mandy and said, 'Do you think it would be OK to give Mr Bell's squirrel a bit of ice-cream? He doesn't seem very happy and I thought it might cheer him up.'

'I shouldn't, Tommy,' replied Mandy. 'It might upset his tummy. Ask Ernie if you can give Sammy a piece of apple or a strawberry. A little bit of fruit is all right for squirrels. They eat berries in the wild, you see.'

Next, Mrs Markham, who lived in one of the pretty terraced cottages just off the lower High Street, came up to Mandy with Bunty, her beagle. 'Bunty's eyes are a bit dry and itchy,' she said. 'I've been bathing them but maybe I should let your mum or dad have a look at them. What do you think, Mandy?'

Mandy bent down and patted the friendly beagle. Then she looked at her eyes. 'Hmm, they do look a bit sore, don't they, Bunty girl!'

'I'll bring her to Animal Ark in the morning,' said Mrs Markham. 'Come on, Bunty, the ice-cream's starting to melt already.'

Then John Hardy, whose father was landlord at the Fox and Goose, asked Mandy if it would be a good idea to put a piece of rock sulphur in his rabbits' drinking water. 'It's supposed to help them keep cool,' he said.

'We'll be lucky to get any ice-cream if people keep treating this patch as the Animal Ark surgery,' whispered James. 'Here's Mrs McFarlane, from the post office. She'll probably ask you to clip her budgie's toenails.'

Mandy grinned. Coming out and talking to people in the village had cheered her up. And Mrs McFarlane *was* going to ask her something. She had that look on her face.

'Hello, Mandy, hello James. Mandy, I hear your grandparents didn't have any success last night! Shame, that. There should be more people like them around, putting themselves out to stop vandalism.'

'We don't get much vandalism in Welford,' James pointed out.

'Ha!' said Mrs McFarlane. 'Throwing litter down is a form of vandalism. Look, there's a couple of lolly wrappers on the ground now.' She stalked over to them, picked them up, then marched back towards the post office.

'She doesn't approve of the ice-cream van,' said Walter Pickard, gazing after her. 'Thinks it takes custom away from the shop.'

'She doesn't open on a Sunday!' said James.

'Doesn't make any difference to her way of thinking,' said Walter. 'And if you two want serving, you'd better get a move on. Everyone else has been served.'

'Bye, Mandy,' called Tommy.

Mandy and James stepped up to the serving hatch. James asked for two giant cups with strawberry sauce and the ice-cream man winked at him, then said solemnly to Mandy, 'I've got this pet gorilla with hairs on his chest. What do you think I should do about it?'

'Pet gorilla!' gasped Mandy, pretending to take him seriously. 'I think you should rub olive oil on his chest ten times a day,' she said.

'Can't catch your girlfriend out, can I?' grinned the ice-cream man, passing out the giant cups, and James turned as red as the strawberry sauce.

Half an hour later, Mandy and James were refusing ice-cream from Mandy's gran. 'We had some from the van and ate it down by the river,' Mandy explained. 'Anyway, Gran, we can't stop. We just popped in to hear about last night.'

'There's nothing to hear,' said Gran. 'We didn't see anything suspicious the whole time.'

'I heard that a policeman almost got attacked,' said Mandy, grinning at James.

'Well,' bristled Gran, 'how was I to know who it was tapping on the camper van window like that?' Mandy and James laughed at the indignant look on Gran's face and, after a moment, she joined in their laughter.

'We did see something you might be interested in, Mandy,' said Grandad, who'd been washing soil off his hands at the kitchen sink. 'A little Lakeland terrier came for a wander around the allotments. About five-thirty this morning it was. We thought it might belong to whoever took the onions. But it was all alone. Ran off when I called out.'

'I can't think of anyone round here with a Lakeland,' said Mandy. 'Did it look like a stray, Grandad?'

'Can't say that it did, Mandy. Looked a bonny little thing, actually.'

'Oh, well, another mystery,' said Mandy. 'And

now we must be going. It's almost time to try Sprite with a bottle again.'

'Don't you go wearing yourself out,' Grandad said fondly. He knew all too well what Mandy was like when a sick animal was involved.

'I'll try not to,' said Mandy.

'I'll take over the day feeds tomorrow and do some of the jobs Mandy usually does. Like cleaning-up after surgery,' said James. 'Mandy can have a bit of a rest then.'

'We'll see about that,' said Mandy. 'Not you feeding her, James; me having a rest, I mean.'

In spite of having been up twice in the night, Mandy was down for breakfast at her usual time.

'How did you get on with feeding Sprite?' her mum asked. 'I looked in at her when I got back from a call-out, about three-thirty. She was sleeping peacefully then.'

'Two o'clock was useless,' Mandy sighed. 'She stood up for a moment when I opened the cage but then she lay back down. She didn't go to sleep, though, and she seemed to be listening to me when I talked to her. Her ears were moving.' Mandy reached for a piece of toast, 'But she didn't take much notice of what I was saying. She just would not get up.

'Then when I came down at five, she was on her feet and quite close to the cage door. I got her bottle ready in double-quick time and she stayed standing when I opened the door. She actually sniffed at the teat a couple of times. I squeezed some milk out and tried pushing the teat quite hard against her mouth. She blinked at me, had another sniff, then down she went.'

Emily Hope shot her daughter a sympathetic smile and put another piece of toast on her plate. 'Eat,' she said firmly. 'I know you're longing to get back to Sprite but you'll be no good to her or any other patient if you pass out from hunger.'

Mandy took one bite then said, 'It was one step closer with Sprite, Mum, I'm sure it was.'

Mr Hope wandered in then, eating a pot of yoghurt and Mandy told of Sprite's progress all over again. Then she turned to her mum. 'Where were you called out to, Mum?' she asked.

'I wondered when you'd ask that!' Emily Hope said with a smile. 'It was a foaling up at Mrs Forsyth's riding stables. Whisper's had a little filly foal. Well, not so little; that was the problem.'

'They're both all right though?' said Mandy.

'They're fine. You'll have to go up and see them, Mandy. Whisper's a very proud mum and the foal is the image of her.'

'Here's Simon,' said Mandy, cocking her head. She would recognise the sound of his old van anywhere. 'I bet he'll be surprised when he sees Sprite. Then he'll start shooting loads of questions at me.'

Simon was Animal Ark's practice nurse and was just as enthusiastic as Mandy and James about wildlife.

'And I expect you're longing to discuss Sprite's case with him!' Mr Hope said seriously.

Mandy nodded and smiled at him. 'I am,' she said. 'And everything's ready for surgery starting so there's half an hour to spare. Unless you need to discuss anything with him?' she added, glancing from him to her mum.

They shook their heads and Mandy hurried out.

Sprite's case, she repeated silently, as she went through the connecting door to the surgery. That sounded so professional. She loved it when her parents spoke to her like that, as though she were already a fully-fledged vet. Mandy was smiling as she went into the annexe.

* * *

James arrived twenty minutes later. He'd brought a large bagful of nettles he'd gathered when he'd taken Blackie for his early morning walk.

He hurried in through the side door which led directly to the residential unit and went straight through to the annexe.

The eager look left his face, his steps faltered and he stood still. He stared at the large, empty cage where Sprite had been. The cage door was open and inside was the bed of nettles and hay. James could still see the hollow in the centre of

them where Sprite had lain. The nettles Mandy had painstakingly threaded through the wire mesh on the door were brown and drooping.

Something must have happened to Sprite, James thought. She must not have made it through the night . . .

He stayed gazing sadly for a moment, then, shoulders hunched, he trudged slowly back outside. He'd hide the bag of fresh nettles in the garage for now. He didn't want Mandy to see them. She'd be upset enough without that.

Six

'Hi, James. They've told you, have they?' James had just finished tucking the bag of nettles out of sight behind some spare tyres at the far end of the garage. At the sound of Mandy's voice he spun round.

'I ... er ...' he began, then he stopped and looked down at his feet. He couldn't quite bring himself to explain how he knew about Sprite.

'You are coming with me, aren't you?' asked Mandy. 'Or were you just getting my bike out for me?'

'Er ... yes,' replied James, playing safe. He'd

no idea what Mandy was talking about but she obviously couldn't bring herself to talk about Sprite just yet, either.

'You don't sound over-enthusiastic,' said Mandy, looking puzzled. 'I thought you'd jump at the chance of going up to Lydia's.'

'It's just . . .' James shrugged and moved towards Mandy's bike which was leaning in its usual place against the garage wall.

'I expect Lydia will be surprised to see us at this time of day,' said Mandy. 'Until I tell her why we're there of course. Well, come on. James, either bring my bike or move over so I can get to it.'

James grabbed the bike and started backing it out. He figured Mandy would talk about Sprite when she was ready.

'Thanks,' said Mandy, taking her bike. 'Where's yours?'

'Outside the residential unit,' James replied.

'OK, we'll go out the front way then and down our lane.'

On their way out, they passed Mrs Markham with her beagle and waved and called a greeting. Then Susan Collins cycled towards them. 'I'm going to fetch some liniment for Prince's leg,' she told Mandy. 'He landed awkwardly when I was jumping him yesterday and I think he'd sprained it. Come round and see him later if you like.'

'Do you remember what a pain she was when she first came to live at The Beeches?' chuckled Mandy as they cycled on. 'Now she's quite nice. And Prince is still my favourite pony.'

James nodded. He was finding it hard to stop thinking about Sprite.

They turned on to the High Street. As they went past the post office Tommy Pickard was just opening the door to go in. 'Hello!' he called. 'How's the little fawn, Mandy?'

'Improving, I think,' Mandy called back. 'We're just going—' She skidded to a halt and asked anxiously, 'James! Are you OK?'

James had jammed his bicycle brakes on so hard that he'd nearly flown over the top of his handlebars. 'What do you mean, Sprite's improving?' he croaked.

'Well, she is,' said Mandy. 'That's why Simon suggested that I asked Mum and Dad if I could put her in the shed.'

James blinked like an owl, then his mouth opened but no words came out.

'James, why are you acting so strangely?' Mandy demanded. 'Do you think we shouldn't have disturbed her? Simon didn't handle her at all, and I carried her out to the shed myself.'

'I thought . . .' James gulped. 'Mandy, I . . . I saw the empty cage and I thought Sprite was dead!'

'Oh, James!' Mandy's eyes were wide with horror and her hand flew up to her mouth. 'What do you think we're going to Lydia's for?' she cried. 'Didn't Mum or Dad tell you?'

James shook his head. 'I didn't see anyone. All I saw was the empty cage.'

'That must have been awful! But why were you in the garage if it wasn't to get my bike out for us going up to High Cross?'

James explained about the bag of nettles. 'So we'll still need them after all,' he said happily. 'And what *are* we going to Lydia's for?'

'Goat's milk,' said Mandy. 'That was Simon's idea too. He reckons Sprite might like it better because it smells and tastes stronger. It's probably more like deer milk.'

'Brilliant!' said James, getting back on the saddle, putting his feet on the pedals and whizzing off before Mandy could catch her breath.

'Come on!' he yelled over his shoulder. 'What are you waiting for?'

They found Lydia Fawcett in the barn, cleaning out the goat pens. She looked up with a smile when she saw them. 'Hello there,' she said. 'This is a surprise. The goats are out in the top meadow, all except Lady Jayne that is,' Lydia said, pointing to one of the pens. 'I think she's getting ready to kid so I'm keeping her in.'

Mandy and James hurried over to Lady Jayne's pen. They loved all Lydia's goats but were particularly attached to Lady Jayne because they'd helped to deliver her twins last time she'd kidded.

'Hello, lovely girl,' said Mandy rubbing the goat's soft nose. 'Are you going to have twins again this time?'

'I reckon it's just a single kid and quite a small one at that,' said Lydia, joining them by the pen and casting a critical gaze over Lady Jayne.

'Lydia, we can't stop,' Mandy went on quickly. 'We've come for some milk, please.'

Lydia Fawcett was never one to waste time with questions. Now, she smiled and said, 'Come on then, I'll get you some.'

'We've got an orphan fawn,' Mandy explained as they hurried across the yard and past the farmhouse to the outbuilding Lydia used as a cool house.

'She's a fallow and we've called her Sprite,' James put in.

'And she's refusing to feed from a bottle,' said Mandy. They walked past the milk churns awaiting collection, towards the lidded buckets containing the milk Lydia kept for herself and a few regular customers.

'I don't know if it's the teat on the bottle or the milk she doesn't like,' Mandy continued. 'We've tried her with cow's milk and Vitamilk . . .'

'So,' said Lydia, 'you reckoned goat's milk might suit her better? I think you're probably right there.'

'It was Simon who suggested it. I wish I'd thought of it myself. We'd have saved some valuable time!' Mandy pursed her lips, breathed deeply and shook her head.

Lydia and James grinned at the look on Mandy's face and James said, 'Even you can't think of everything, you know!'

'I'll give you enough milk to last a couple of

days,' said Lydia, ladling it into sterile jars as she spoke. 'If Lady Jayne has kidded, I might even take a walk down to Animal Ark tomorrow afternoon. I'd love to see Sprite for myself. And, of course, I'll bring some more milk if I come.'

'That would be great, Lydia!' Mandy responded enthusiastically, and James threw her a puzzled glance. He'd expected Mandy to protest and say they'd come up for the milk themselves. He was certain she'd be longing to see Lady Jayne's new kid. But Sprite was clearly her priority.

Lydia's phone rang just then. It was only recently she'd been able to afford to have a telephone put in; it was a cordless one and she kept the handset in her pocket when she was working outside. She pulled it out with a flourish.

'We'll go now, Lydia,' Mandy said quickly, picking up the jars. Lydia nodded and pressed the 'talk' button.

'Wait, Mandy,' said Lydia. 'It's for you. Simon,' she added, holding the handset out.

'Sprite!' gasped Mandy, her eyes widening in alarm as she grabbed the handset from Lydia and pressed it to her ear.

Seven

'You know, I still can't believe it,' said Mandy. It was three hours since Simon had phoned her at Lydia's and she, her mum and dad and James were sitting round the kitchen table eating lunch.

Mandy munched on a lettuce leaf. 'I really expected the worst when Lydia told me Simon was on the phone. And then when he told me to get back as quickly as possible because Sprite was maa-ing and he thought maybe she was hungry . . . I was really slow to take it in.'

'You weren't so slow once you had taken it in,' said James. 'I think we should go in *The Guinness*

Book of Records for cycling in the quickest time ever from High Cross to here.'

'And to think,' Mandy went on, 'she gulped the bottle of goat's milk down like she'd been doing it all her life.'

Mandy waved a celery stick around, 'Did Sprite feel happier in the shed, or would she have decided to feed anyway or was it because it was goat's milk?'

'Mandy!' Emily Hope protested, laughing, 'just calm down and get on with your lunch.'

Mandy grinned back at her mum and said, 'You're right, Mum. It doesn't really matter why Sprite's decided to feed, it's enough that she has.'

'Talking of animals feeding,' said Adam Hope, raising his eyebrows in question.

Mandy stretched across the table to waggle a breadstick at him. 'Dad! I never forget about my rabbits, no matter what else is going on.'

'Just checking.' He gave an apologetic smile which turned to a triumphant one as he grabbed the breadstick and popped it in his mouth.

'Adam!' scolded his wife. 'Your table manners are terrible!'

Mandy giggled delightedly. 'Actually, I fed my

rabbits just after I'd moved Sprite to the shed.
Before we went to Lydia's.'

'And I went down to play with them when we
came back. While Mandy was feeding Sprite,'
said James.

'We haven't forgotten Blackie, either,' said
Mandy. 'James and I thought we'd take him for
a walk. After we've washed up the lunch things,'
she added quickly. 'And we'll be back by three.
James can feed Sprite and I'll help with afternoon surgery.'

'That sounds all right,' Mr Hope agreed. 'Your
mum and I have both got a couple of routine
farm calls to make but other than that,' he
tapped the wooden table, 'there's nothing until
surgery time.'

'There is one thing,' Emily Hope said, looking
meaningfully at Mandy. 'Now that it looks as if
Sprite is going to survive—'

'I know what you're going to say, Mum,'
Mandy interrupted. 'And James and I are working on it. Aren't we, James?'

James nodded, trying not to look too puzzled.
Some days things seemed like they were going
much too fast for him. And today was one of
those days.

He still hadn't got round to asking Mandy why she'd been so eager for Lydia to come to Animal Ark instead of the two of them going there. And now, he and Mandy were working on something, but he didn't know what!

Mandy grinned at him and shook her head, warning him not to comment, then she got up and started clearing the lunch things away. 'Last one to the sink washes up!' Seeing as she was almost there, it was an unfair challenge.

'I prefer to wash anyway,' James told Mandy's parents. 'The one who dries has to put away as well.'

James smiled as he got up to go over to the sink. He was just filling it with water when there was a quick knock on the kitchen door. Jean Knox popped her head inside.

'Sorry to disturb you,' she said, looking at Mandy's parents, 'but Ernie Bell is in Reception and wonders if he could have a word?'

Mandy and James glanced worriedly at each other. Emily Hope rose from the table and said 'I'll come and see him, Jean.'

'It's probably something to do with the kitchen cupboards Ernie's making for us,' said Adam Hope, pouring himself a second cup of tea.

'I bet it's something to do with Sammy,' said Mandy. 'He's been a bit miserable the last two days.'

'Go through and find out what's going on,' suggested James. 'I'll finish off in here.'

Mandy shook her head. She hadn't helped out at all today; the least she could do was stay and clear up. 'No,' she said, 'we'll do it together, James. Mum will come and tell us if there's anything wrong.'

'I'd better get going,' Mr Hope drained his cup and walked over to bring it to the sink.

'Where are you going, Dad?' Mandy asked, her mind clearly on what was going on in the surgery rather than on his answer.

'To the moon, to see the cow who jumped over it,' he replied.

'Oh, right,' Mandy said vaguely. Then she realised what her dad had said and giggled.

'So you are with us, after all!' he teased. 'No, I'm going up to Burnside Farm to check on Clover and her new calf.'

'Why? Is there a problem?' Mandy was giving her dad her full attention now.

'Not that I know of, but it was Clover's first calf and she did have a rough time of it.'

Mandy nodded and smiled at her dad. She loved the way he kept an eye on all of the 'new mums' as they called them, just in case anything was going wrong. 'I'll see you both later,' he added, as he went out.

Emily Hope hadn't returned by the time Mandy and James had finished. 'We'll go through now and see what's happening,' Mandy decided.

There was no sign of her mum or Ernie Bell in the reception area. Jean Knox was on the telephone and Mandy waited impatiently while the receptionist wrote down the caller's name and address in the home visits book.

'Right,' said Jean, when she'd finished on the phone. 'You've come for the antiseptic cream to take to the vicarage, have you?'

'No, we came to see Mum,' said Mandy.

'She isn't here,' Jean told her, sticking her pen behind her ear – where no doubt she'd forget all about it. Jean was the most forgetful person Mandy had ever met.

In spite of her impatience, Mandy turned to grin at James. Then she turned back to face Jean. 'Do you know where she is, please, Jean?'

'I thought you knew. Didn't she tell you where

she was going when she asked you to take this cream . . .' Jean picked up a small wrapped package, '. . . to the vicarage. Oh, no, wait a minute, I remember now. She asked me to give you the message. That's all right then.' She pushed the package into Mandy's hand.

'I'm to take this to the vicarage, am I?' asked Mandy.

'Yes, Mr Hadcroft phoned just before your mum left to go and look at Mr Bell's squirrel. Jemima is nibbling at her tail again and making it sore.' Some time back, the vicar's cat had been in an accident which had meant having to have part of her tail removed. Since then she'd developed the habit of nibbling the shortened tip.

'And Mum has gone to look at Sammy?' prompted Mandy.

'Yes, Mr Bell says the squirrel isn't himself. He's eating and drinking as usual but his movements seem a bit twitchy; that's what Mr Bell said.'

Jean leaned confidingly over the desk, 'Ernie Bell seemed a touch twitchy himself,' she whispered. 'Scowled the whole time he was here then marched out with your mum without so much as a goodbye.'

'He'll be OK when Mum's checked Sammy over,' said Mandy. 'We'll go round this evening and see them both then.'

'Yes. What if I go and fetch Blackie now and meet you at the vicarage?' James suggested. 'Then we can take the footpath across Farmer Redpath's field, and go down to the riverbank.'

'And be back here in time for Sprite's next feed and afternoon surgery,' said Mandy.

Mandy lay flat on her back, her eyes closed against the bright sun, listening to the gentle burbling of the river as it meandered lazily over the pebbles.

James was studying a family of ladybirds he'd spotted in a clump of tall-growing grass. He suddenly remembered a snippet of information he'd stored away in his mind.

'I read somewhere that millions of ladybirds hibernate every year in the Sierra Nevada mountains,' said James. 'People are paid to collect them and they're put in cold storage until spring. Then garden centres all over America sell them as a natural pest control.'

'I'll try to remember that,' Mandy said drowsily. 'It's sure to come in useful one day.'

James grinned then shrugged. He'd thought it was interesting anyway!

Just then, Blackie came back from his exploration of the river. He bounded happily over to Mandy and shook the water from his fur.

'Ouch! Blackie!' protested Mandy, shooting up into a sitting position. 'You'd need millions of ladybirds to control you, you pest!'

Blackie wagged his tail and started to lick Mandy's bare arms. Then he pulled at something sticking out of the pocket in her shorts.

'Oh, James,' said Mandy, gently pushing Blackie's big head out of the way, 'I forgot to show you these. On my way to the vicarage I called in on Miss Davy to thank her for helping us with Sprite. She gave me these photos she took a few days ago.'

'Squirrels on her garden wall,' said James, crouching down beside Mandy to look at the photos. 'What are they eating?' He held one photo up to peer closely at it.

'Don't know,' Mandy replied, 'I was going to ask Miss Davy that but someone arrived for a music lesson so I didn't get round to it.'

'That reminds me,' said James. 'There's a couple of things I've been meaning to ask you.'

'Mmm?' said Mandy, brushing some drops of water from her arm. 'Oh, heck, I'm getting sunburned.'

'Well, first-off—' James broke off to stare in alarm at Blackie who was whining loudly and rubbing his nose furiously on the ground.

'I think he's been stung!' said Mandy, bending down beside the dog and taking his face in her hands. 'Here, James.' She fumbled in her pocket and brought out a tissue. 'Go and wet this. The cold will help relieve the sting, then we'll get him back to Animal Ark. Simon will be there even if Mum and Dad aren't back.'

Eight

Blackie lay on the examining table and whined as Simon ran careful fingers over his nose and muzzle. 'It's just below his nose, I think,' Mandy's finger circled the area. 'That's the part he was rubbing on the ground.'

'I don't think whatever it was left the sting in,' said Simon. 'I can't really see where he was stung, and there's no sign of any swelling.' He lifted Blackie's lip and looked at the inside of his mouth then examined his tongue and throat. 'Nothing here, either.'

James nodded tensely and shoved his glasses further on to his nose.

Blackie whined again and looked at them with sad eyes. 'You're a bit of a fraud,' Mandy told him. 'You're enjoying all this attention; your wagging tail is giving you away, boy.'

'There's definitely nothing inside his mouth, James,' assured Simon. 'I'll take a look at his ears and eyes just to be on the safe side, but I don't think there's any cause for alarm.

'Right,' said Simon after a few seconds, 'I declare this dog to be in fine fettle. Come on, down you get, boy. I'll give you some antiseptic cream to rub on where we think he was stung, James. That should do the trick.'

'Simon, if an animal was stung and wasn't treated could the reaction to the sting make it go twitchy?' asked Mandy.

'You're thinking of Ernie's squirrel, Mandy?' said Simon. 'It is one thing your mum will look for.' Blackie woofed and trotted to the treatment room door. 'This is probably her now.' Simon wiped the treatment table down with disinfectant. 'You can ask her for yourself.'

Mandy glanced at the clock. 'Yes, then it will be time for Sprite's feed.'

'Hello, Blackie! What are you doing here?' Emily Hope's voice floated in to them and Mandy and James thanked Simon and went out to tell her.

'Any news about Sammy?' Mandy said. '*Is* he ill, Mum?'

'Not ill exactly, Mandy. But he isn't at all himself. Could be he's getting muscular cramps; that would fit with his occasional twitchiness. But we'd have to ask *why* he's getting them. Anyway, I've given Ernie some vitamin tonic and we'll keep and eye on him.'

'You don't think something's frightened Sammy, like the fox did that time?'

'No. Sammy isn't in shock; those symptoms

are fairly easy to diagnose. And now, I've just about time for a cold drink before surgery. Are you helping, Mandy?'

Mandy glanced at James. Did he want to feed Sprite or was he still worried about Blackie?

James grinned. 'There doesn't seem much wrong with Blackie now; he's tearing round the garden. Just set me going with Sprite, Mandy, then you can leave me to it.'

'I saw Gran on my way home,' said Emily Hope. 'There's been no sign of the onion thief and she told me to tell you and James to go round for tea. She's been baking all afternoon. I don't know where she gets the energy from in this heat!'

'I'm sure James and I will find enough energy to do some serious eating,' said Mandy. 'I'm starving already. And I hope Sprite's hungry, too,' she added. 'Let's go and make up her bottle, James.'

'It sounds as if Sprite *might* be hungry,' James said as they walked towards the shed. 'Listen, Mandy, she's maa-ing again.'

When they opened the shed door, Sprite went right up to Mandy and pushed her velvety nose against her hand. 'Oh, Sprite!' gasped Mandy, bending down to look at the fawn. She resisted the temptation to stroke the soft, gingery hair between Sprite's ears. 'We mustn't turn you into a pet. And, no, I haven't got your bottle. James has.'

'Maa,' said Sprite. And, as if she'd understood Mandy's words, she turned her head to look at James.

'Come on, girl,' he whispered, holding the bottle out. 'Come and drink your milk. That's right. There's a good fawn.'

One problem over and another one about to start, Mandy thought as she went to help with surgery. They needed to figure out what would happen to Sprite once she was able to leave Animal Ark. Perhaps James and she could talk about it on the way to Gran's, Mandy thought as she went back inside.

But they didn't get to Mandy's grandparents' for tea. Just as surgery ended, Lydia Fawcett phoned. Lady Jayne was having problems and could someone come up?

'It must be bad for Lydia to ask that,' Mandy threw a worried look at her mum. 'There isn't much she can't handle herself.'

'Tell her I'll be there within quarter of an hour,

Jean,' said Emily Hope. 'If you and James want to come, Mandy, you've got three minutes!'

Mandy flew out to fetch James. He was just coming out of the shed. 'Sprite drank every single drop,' he said proudly, showing Mandy the empty feeding bottle. 'And I've cleaned her out as well. She's getting very friendly now, Mandy. We'll have to be careful about that.'

'Yes, I was thinking the same thing myself,' Mandy agreed quickly. 'But Lydia's just phoned. There's a problem with Lady Jayne. We're going up to High Cross Farm!'

An hour later, Lydia shook her head and glanced apologetically at Emily Hope. 'I should have realised what it was,' she said. 'I've never seen it happen but I do vaguely remember my father talking about it. Must have been a long time back; he's been dead a good few years now.'

'I've never actually seen it before,' said Mrs Hope. 'The old country name for it is "cloud-burst".'

'So it was a false pregnancy, Mum?' asked Mandy.

Mrs Hope nodded. 'Lady Jayne looked and acted as though she was in kid, right down to the last stage. But all she'd been carrying was fluid.'

'I thought she was carrying a *small* kid,' Lydia sighed. 'I never dreamed she wasn't carrying one at all.'

'Will Lady Jayne be all right though, Mrs Hope?' asked James.

'Yes, she'll be fine, James.' Emily Hope leaned over to rub Lady Jayne's head, 'Maybe just a bit puzzled for a while, but she'll soon forget, won't you, girl!'

'I'm sorry to have dragged you up here on a wild goose chase,' Lydia apologised again. 'I'll leave Lady Jayne to rest and get on with milking the others. It's more than time; they'll be getting restless.'

Emily Hope glanced at Mandy and James. 'Ready, you two?'

'Is it OK if James and I stay and help with the milking?' Mandy asked. 'Sprite won't need feeding for another couple of hours yet. I'll phone Gran and ask if it'll be OK for us to visit tomorrow instead.'

'Right, I'll get back then. James, would you like me to drop Blackie off home for you?'

'Thanks, Mrs Hope. That would be a big help,'

James replied. Then he and Mandy dashed off after Lydia to bring the goats in for milking.

It took them an hour to finish milking. The churns of milk were placed under running water before being taken to the cool house. After that, Mandy and James decided to go and see Lady Jayne before they went back to Welford.

'You do realise don't you, girl, that you've messed up my plan by not having a kid?' Mandy's eyes were worried as she petted the goat.

'What do you mean, Mandy? How has she?'

Mandy explained. 'This morning when Lydia said she thought Lady Jayne would only have one kid I jumped at the idea of Lydia coming to see Sprite.'

'I kept meaning to ask why you were so keen,' said James.

'Well,' Mandy sighed, 'when Lady Jayne had twin kids, she fed them both for the first couple of weeks, right?'

'Right,' agreed James.

'So I thought if Lydia came to see the fawn, she might fall in love with her and agree to my plan.'

'What plan?' James asked.

'To get Lady Jayne to foster Sprite. To feed her for a couple of weeks, along with her own kid, before we release her. That way, Sprite wouldn't have got too used to us or to being kept indoors, either!'

'It's a brilliant idea, Mandy,' said James.

'But no good now.' Mandy pulled a face. 'No kid for Lady Jayne, no milk for Sprite, see?'

'We'll just have to keep bottle-feeding Sprite,' said James. 'At least she's willing to let us do that now. We'll just have to make sure she doesn't get too attached to us. She might not, not in only a couple of weeks.'

'Mmm. It's a shame though,' said Mandy sadly. 'Lady Jayne's such a gentle goat. I'm sure she would have accepted a little orphan fawn.'

'There are two things wrong with what you've just said, Mandy Hope.' Lydia's amused voice came from the barn door. 'I couldn't help overhearing,' she added, walking forward to join them.

'It wasn't a secret,' said Mandy. 'Just an idea I'd had.' She gave another sigh then asked curiously, 'So what was I wrong about, Lydia?'

'Lady Jayne will still come into milk just as though she had kidded,' replied Lydia.

For a moment, Mandy's hopes soared. Her plan might be possible after all. That's if Lydia agreed, of course.

But then Lydia continued, 'You did say Sprite is a fallow, right?'

Mandy and James nodded.

'Well,' said Lydia, 'you can't release her in a couple of weeks then.'

'But she isn't a newborn,' explained Mandy. 'Dad thinks she's four or five weeks old now. She can be weaned—'

'*Weaned* by the time she's six or seven weeks, yes!' Lydia interrupted. 'But not released, Mandy. Fallow fawns stay with the doe for over a year. Muntjac deer are independent at two months or so but not the fallow!'

'Mum and Dad never said!' gasped Mandy.

'You probably didn't give them the chance!' said James. 'Or maybe they thought you knew.'

'That's true,' admitted Mandy. 'I wanted so much to sort everything out myself, I stopped Mum every time she started to talk about it.'

She and James gazed worriedly at each other. This was terrible! What were they going to do? They couldn't keep Sprite in Animal Ark's garden shed for a year!

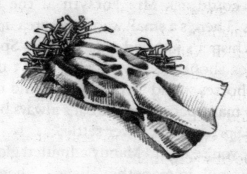

Nine

'James, we've got a very serious problem here,' Mandy said at last.

James nodded and shoved his glasses further on to his nose. 'What about Betty Hilder's animal sanctuary?' he suggested.

'No, we need somewhere where Sprite could have a sort of organised freedom,' Mandy replied slowly. 'And someone who can keep an eye on her without making her too dependent.'

'Somewhere with other animals so Sprite won't get lonely,' said James. 'And maybe a few trees or a small wood . . . I mean, a deer's natural home is a forest.'

'We could ask Mrs Forsyth at the riding stables. There's a small woodland area up there and Whisper's just had a foal. Maybe Sprite—'

James shook his head. 'That won't do. All those horses would terrify Sprite. And there'd be too many people around; it's always busy up there. Sprite would never settle.'

'Yes, you're right,' Mandy admitted gloomily.

They sank into another silence. Then Lydia spoke.

'I've thought it over,' she said, 'and although I can't offer much in the way of trees . . .'

'Do you mean Sprite *could* come here?' said Mandy, hardly daring to hope. 'Even though she'd have to stay for . . .'

'For a lot longer than two or three weeks,' James finished the sentence for her.

'We could certainly see if Lady Jayne and the rest of the herd would be willing to accept her,' Lydia replied. 'And, of course, if Sprite will accept them.'

'Oh, Lydia,' gulped Mandy. She felt like throwing her arms around Lydia and hugging her. Instead, she turned and hugged Lady Jayne.

Lydia smiled across at James and, blushing a bit, he mumbled, 'High Cross will be a terrific home for Sprite. I'm sure she'll be happy here.'

'When can we bring her?' Mandy asked eagerly. 'It's not that we're in a hurry to get rid of her, Lydia. But it would be better if she didn't get too used to us. And the sooner she's here, the sooner we'll know if it's going to work. And . . . thanks, Lydia!' she ended breathlessly.

'I should think the day after tomorrow,' said Lydia, her eyes twinkling. 'Lady Jayne will be rested enough then. But don't thank me yet,' she laughed. 'If we want Lady Jayne to feed the fawn, there'll be a bit more to it than just bringing her, Mandy. We'll need to do something to attract them to each other. Under normal circumstances mothers and their young recognise each other by smell.'

'You mean we have to make them smell like each other?' asked Mandy looking puzzled.

'But how do we do that?' asked James.

'There's only one way I can think of,' said Lydia.

'Uh-oh! I think I know what you're getting at,' said Mandy. 'I've got a feeling we're in for a rather messy job, James. I think we'll have to rub Sprite all over with soiled straw from Lady Jayne's pen. Is that right, Lydia?'

'Afraid so,' Lydia smiled. 'And Lady Jayne will need rubbing with the fawn's soiled straw, too.'

'Do you think it *will* work? asked Mandy.

'We'll have to wait and see,' said Lydia.

'In the meantime,' said James, pointing to his watch, 'it's still down to us to feed Sprite. And her feed's due in about half an hour.'

They said goodbye to Lydia and thanked her again. Then they hurried off, chattering happily and making plans for getting Sprite to High Cross on Wednesday. They went past Upper Welford Hall, then past Beacon House, waving to Imogen Parker Smythe who was picking dandelion leaves for her two rabbits.

'I'll race you down to the bridge!' James challenged at the top of the steep hill. He sped away with Mandy pounding behind him and they arrived at the bridge together.

They spotted Ernie Bell and Walter Pickard sitting outside the Fox and Goose and went across to say hello and to ask Ernie how Sammy was.

'He still isn't himself,' said Ernie. 'Didn't seem to want to come with me when I came out; and you know how he likes riding on my shoulder.

Come and see for yourself, if you like.'

'He's right worried about that squirrel of his,' said Walter Pickard quietly, as Ernie got up and started moving away.

'Are you coming then?' Ernie demanded testily, glancing back at James and Mandy.

They smiled at Walter and quickly followed Ernie round the back of the pub to his cottage garden.

Sammy was in his run, sitting on a sawn-off tree-trunk. Usually, when anyone approached, the squirrel would dart to the wire netting, scamper up it, sit on one of the supports and hold his paw out for a titbit.

'See what I mean?' said Ernie, shaking his head. 'It isn't like Sammy at all, not coming to greet us.'

'Come on, Sammy,' said Mandy. 'Come and say hello.'

James called him, too, and eventually Sammy came over to them. But he didn't chatter and his eyes weren't as bright as usual. He did take the nuts Ernie gave him, though; moving back to the tree-trunk to eat them.

'Well, at least he's eating,' said Mandy. 'Maybe it's just the hot weather making him feel a bit tired and lazy.'

'Maybe,' agreed Ernie. 'And the vitamin tonic your mum gave us might buck him up in a day or two.'

Mandy nodded. 'I'm sure she'll pop in tomorrow to look at him.'

Then she and James said goodbye to Sammy and Ernie and hurried off to Animal Ark.

'Dad's gone to a meeting and Mum's been called out,' said Mandy, quickly reading the note her mum had left her. 'I can't wait to tell them Lydia's offered to have Sprite at High Cross.'

'Tomorrow will be her last full day here,' said James, as he and Mandy went to get Sprite's bottle ready.

'Yes, I've worked it out,' said Mandy, 'and we've only got ten more bottle feeds, then . . .' she crossed her fingers, '. . . Lady Jayne will be feeding her.'

'I'll miss most of tomorrow's feeds,' said James. 'Dad's taking me to that computer exhibition in Walton. I'll try and be back in time for tea at your gran's, though.'

'That's why my tummy feels so funny,' said Mandy. 'We haven't eaten anything for hours.

Do you want to feed Sprite on your own while I make us something to eat, James?'

Mandy put some jacket potatoes to cook in the microwave. She had just set the timer when the front door bell rang. It was Miss Davy.

'I was hoping you might be in, Mandy,' she said. 'I've just found out that an old and dear friend of mine is going into hospital for a rather serious operation. Afterwards, all being well, he'll be going to the coast to get well again.'

Mandy nodded, guessing what was coming next.

'I thought perhaps you might know of someone who could give his pets a loving and happy home,' Eileen Davy continued. 'I brought a photograph of them with me in case you were in.'

She reached under the pile of magazines in her old-fashioned basket and drew out a paper wallet. She selected a photo and passed it to Mandy. 'There, dear.'

Mandy looked at the photograph. It was of three goldfish in a rather large and splendid glass bowl.

Mandy held back a giggle. 'Nobody comes to mind straight away,' she said, 'but I'll think about

it. And I'll put the photo and a card on Animal
Ark's notice-board.'

'Thank you, Mandy.'

'By the way,' said Mandy. 'That photograph
of the squirrels you gave me; do you know what
they're eating?'

'Yes. Deers' antlers,' Eileen Davy replied. 'I
didn't know what they were myself. One of my
pupils told me when I showed him the photograph. He says it's usually the young squirrels
who collect and eat cast-off antlers. He doesn't
know why they do it, just that they do.'

'I'll ask Mum and Dad about it,' said Mandy.
Eileen Davy nodded and bustled away.

But it was late when Mandy's parents came
home. Mandy was so busy telling them about
Lydia offering to have Sprite and making plans
for taking her to High Cross, she completely
forgot to ask.

Two days later, James arrived nice and early at
Animal Ark. It was Sprite's big day. By nine
o'clock they were up at Lydia's, busily rubbing
Lady Jayne with the soiled straw they'd brought
with them from Sprite's shed.

An hour or so later, Adam Hope came to fetch

them, and the bags of straw from Lady Jayne's pen. Before long Mandy and James were putting their rubber gloves on again, ready to rub Sprite down.

'I can just imagine it when we go back to school next week,' said James. 'Mr Adams will ask, "And what did you do during half-term, James?" And I'll reply, "Well, Sir, the day that stands out in my mind most is Wednesday. Mandy and I spent the whole day rubbing a fawn with soiled straw from a goat's pen." '

'Shut up and keep rubbing!' Mandy spoke like someone out of an old gangster movie.

'This is one of the smelliest jobs I've ever done.'

'But it'll be worth it, James!' Mandy kneeled back on her heels and gazed happily at the little fawn. Sprite moved her head and turned soft golden-brown eyes on Mandy as if to say, 'Keep rubbing! I was enjoying it!'

Mandy knew they were taking a risk by handling Sprite this much, rubbing her down with the soiled straw. Especially as Sprite was clearly enjoying it. 'It probably reminds her of when her mother used to lick her,' Mandy said aloud.

'But Sprite's mother would have licked Sprite

to clean her,' James pointed out. 'We're rubbing Sprite to make her smell.'

'Yes,' Mandy agreed. 'To make her smell as much like a goat as possible so that Lady Jayne won't reject her. Because if *she* accepts her then the others will as well. Anyway, if this is what Lydia thinks it takes to help it work, I'm all for it.'

'You'd have done whatever Lydia suggested,' James said good-naturedly, 'and probably persuaded me to do it as well. I'm just glad it was nothing worse than this. But off-hand I can't *think* of anything worse,' he added, wrinkling his nose.

They worked in silence for a while, their gloved hands rhythmically rubbing clumps of straw over Sprite's body and legs. Sprite swayed slightly from side to side, her head up and her eyes closed.

'OK,' said Mandy at last. 'I'll go and dump the rest of this straw in the back of the Land-rover on a plastic sheet, ready for Sprite to lie in on her journey to her new home. And you keep rubbing!'

James nodded. 'Thanks a lot, Mandy,' he said.

* * *

An hour later Sprite was safely within a goat pen in Lydia's barn. Mandy, Mrs Hope, James and Lydia stood by the barn doorway watching as Sprite gazed round with curious eyes. Occasionally, the little fawn lifted her head and sniffed the air, or pawed at the straw around her feet.

'I think we should leave her to it for a while,' said Lydia.

'It looks as if the first stage has been successful, doesn't it?' Mandy said as they crossed the yard. 'The journey here didn't worry her at all and she seems to be accepting her new surroundings.'

'Yes. So far, so good,' agreed Lydia.

'There's a long way to go yet, Mandy,' Emily Hope warned. 'Sprite might panic when she sees the goats. Or even if she decides she likes the goats they might not be willing to accept a fawn into the herd.'

Lydia nodded as they went into the kitchen. 'It's not so much the feeding we need to worry about. I could keep her on the bottle if necessary. But if the goats turn against her, they'd make her life a misery.'

'Either way,' James said slowly, 'if Sprite

doesn't take to the goats or they don't take to her, we'll have to think of something else.'

'It will work,' Mandy said confidently. 'It will probably take time and patience but it will work.'

It's got to, she added silently. *Because I can't think of anywhere else for Sprite to go if it doesn't!*

Ten

'I do think it could work or I wouldn't have offered,' said Lydia. 'But I just want you to be aware of the possibility of it not working, Mandy.'

'There, Mum,' Mandy smiled triumphantly. 'At least one thing is clear. You've just heard it from Lydia's own lips. She offered. I didn't talk her into it.'

'Aye, but as my old dad used to say,' Lydia treated Mandy to one of her rare smiles, 'there's more than one way of knitting a sock. Or, in this case, more than one way of getting someone to do something. It was the look on your face that did it, Mandy!'

'Mmm! I know exactly which look you're talking about,' said Mandy's mum. 'And now, if you're sure you're happy about everything, Lydia, I'd better go and do some house visits.'

'If you two are staying,' Lydia said to Mandy and James, 'you can make yourselves useful. Houdini and Monty could do with a good grooming. Those two billy-goats get messier than all the nannies put together. When you've done that we'll bring Lady Jayne and Olivia to the barn. We'll walk them slowly past Sprite a couple of times and see how they all react.'

'Great!' said Mandy. 'I'll see you later, Mum.'

'It's my yoga class tonight, remember, Mandy. So I might not be in when you get home.'

'I'll be home in time to make supper for when you come back,' Mandy called as her mum hurried towards the Land-rover.

'Right, I'll tell your dad,' Emily Hope called back. 'And good luck, all of you.'

'Right. We'll take Lady Jayne and Olivia into the barn now,' decided Lydia when James and Mandy returned from grooming the billy-goats in the top meadow. 'And, unless things get unpleasant, which I don't think they will; we won't interfere. OK?'

Mandy and James nodded, both too anxious to speak. Lydia, though, seemed her usual calm and competent self as she led the two goats through the barn door and towards Sprite's pen.

There was a lot of sideways looking, a lot of sniffing then a couple of little bleating noises. *Like they're asking each other, 'Who is this?'* thought Mandy, her eyes going from Sprite to the goats as though she were watching a tennis match.

When Lady Jayne bobbed her head through the little keyhole gap in the door of Sprite's pen, Mandy grabbed hold of James's arm and clutched it hard. Slowly, making little sniffing noises, Sprite bent her head right down to the gap and . . .

Mandy almost gasped aloud. For three or four seconds, Sprite and Lady Jayne rubbed noses. Then suddenly, Sprite backed away, staring wide-eyes at the gap. But when Lady Jayne withdrew her head from the gap, Sprite moved forward again, rested her head on top of the pen door and stared hard at Lady Jayne.

Olivia, as though bored with the whole thing, wandered off to find a haynet to nibble. A couple of minutes later, Lady Jayne pawed at Sprite's door then turned round to look at Lydia.

Mandy felt sure the goat was asking to be let in to the pen. She and James looked at each other then turned their eyes to Lydia. Neither of them dared breathe, let alone speak!

Lydia moved forward and opened the pen door.

Lady Jayne tossed her head and walked in. She went right up to Sprite and sniffed her all over. The little fawn stood there all still and big-eyed, though Mandy was sure she could see her trembling.

Then Lady Jayne licked the top of Sprite's front leg. Sprite made a strange little murmuring sound and bent her head to rub her face against the goat's. When Mandy saw the fawn's little tail wagging she felt a single tear trickling down her cheek; and even James gave a small sniff.

But, all of a sudden, Lady Jayne put her head down and butted poor Sprite so hard she fell down. And after that, the goat backed herself out of the pen and strutted over to stand outside her own pen.

'No harm done,' Lydia said quietly as she

closed the door of Sprite's pen. 'Look, she's getting up now.'

Mandy gulped and nodded. James took his glasses off and rubbed his eyes.

'It needn't mean Lady Jayne has taken against Sprite. She may have just been showing the little fawn who's boss,' Lydia added comfortingly. 'That's right, isn't it, girl?'

After asking James and Mandy to bring Olivia, Lydia led Lady Jayne back outside.

'Honestly, Mum, it was heart-breaking!' said Mandy. It was the Hopes' suppertime and

Mandy had just finished telling them all about Sprite and Lady Jayne.

'I think it sounds quite promising, Mandy,' Adam Hope comforted. 'It sounds as if Lady Jayne was just showing her authority when she butted poor Sprite.'

Mandy's face brightened. 'Anyway, Lydia's going to bottle-feed Sprite tonight and tomorrow, making sure Lady Jayne can see what she's doing. Then she'll try letting them get close to each other again.'

'So that means no Mandy again all day tomorrow, does it?' asked her mum.

'No, it doesn't, Mum. Lydia thinks it will be best if I stay away and leave her to it. She'll phone if she needs me. Well, she'll phone anyway to let us know how things are going.' Mandy let out a mournful sigh and her parents smiled sympathetically.

'We'll have to find you some interesting jobs to do to keep your mind off what's happening up at High Cross,' said Mr Hope, stroking his beard thoughtfully.

'Yes, you will!' agreed Mandy. 'James is going to his cousin's in York for the day, so I'll really need something to keep me occupied.'

* * *

Mandy was up early the next morning. It was cooler today so she put her rabbits in their run to hop and leap around while she cleaned their cage out.

After a while her dad called her in for breakfast. 'Just the two of us, I'm afraid,' he said. 'Your mum's up at Bleakfell Hall. Pandora has got tummy ache and Mrs Ponsonby is imagining the worst. I don't think it will be anything more serious than too much pampering, though!

'What are your plans, love?' he continued. 'I *think* we've got a busy morning's surgery, but I can't find the appointment book. Jean seems to have hidden it!'

'I'll look for it after breakfast, Dad. I know most of the places Jean puts things.'

Mandy soon found the appointment book. Her dad was right; it *was* going to be a busy surgery.

'Almost every single dog and cat in Welford seems to be coming for their booster injections!' she said aloud.

'Talking to yourself, Mandy?' teased Simon, as he walked in. 'You're getting as bad as Jean.'

'I heard that!' said Jean, who was just behind him.

'I saw Ernie Bell on my way here,' Jean added. 'He's still worried about Sammy. I said I'd ask your mum to call round again, Mandy. And I saw Eileen Davy as well. She wanted to know if anyone had asked about the goldfish yet.'

'Have they?' asked Mandy.

Jean shook her head and Mandy sighed. 'I put the photo and the "home wanted" card right in the middle of the notice-board,' she said.

'It's a good photo,' said Simon, walking over to the board for a closer look. 'Did Eileen Davy take it?'

'Yes,' said Mandy. 'And I've just remembered something I meant to ask Mum and Dad. But you might know the answer, Simon.'

Mandy told him about the photograph of squirrels Eileen Davy had taken. 'They were eating deers' antlers,' she said. 'Someone told her that young squirrels do that. But we don't know why.'

'I think it could be for the mineral content,' Simon said thoughtfully. 'Antlers are like bone. They contain quite a lot of calcium.'

'Do you think deers' antlers might be able to help Sammy?' asked Mandy. 'I know Mum's given him a tonic but . . .'

'Have a word with your mum or dad first,' said Simon. 'It might be worth a try, Mandy. You wouldn't have to give Sammy many pieces, though,' he warned her. 'Too much calcium in a diet can be just as bad as not enough.'

'Well, if Mum says it's OK, I know exactly what I'm going to do after I've helped with morning surgery,' Mandy said happily.

A couple of hours later, Mandy set off for the little forest behind Eileen Davy's house to search for bits of shed-off antlers. She knew it might take some time to find any; they were sure to be well scattered.

She searched the tracks and undergrowth diligently and eventually came across quite a long piece of antler. Soon after she found two smaller bits. She had just decided to call it a day when she turned on to another narrow track which wound its way upwards over a small but steep rise.

She had to go carefully; the whole place seemed to be potted with rabbit-holes. After catching her foot in one, Mandy stooped to rub it. That was when she heard a muffled sound; a whining noise, quickly followed by a series of panicky yaps. It could only mean one thing. A dog was stuck down one of the rabbit-holes!

Mandy went down on her hands and knees, crawled to the nearest burrow then lay flat on her stomach and peered down it.

'Where are you? Good dog!' she called. 'Good dog!'

Mandy's words met with no response; not at the first burrow or the following four she peered into and called down.

She kneeled up and rubbed grubby hands over her sweatshirt. Then she put her fingers to her mouth and let out a piercing whistle.

The whining and the yapping started again; more frantic this time and quite close. 'Keep it up!' Mandy encouraged loudly. 'Good dog; where are you then?'

Mandy stretched out on her stomach again and put her ear to the ground. The dog was still whining. Mandy wriggled closer and closer to the sound. It was getting louder now . . .

'Yes,' muttered Mandy, 'round about here.' She groped around with her hands, found a stick and struck it in the ground above the spot where the whining was loudest. Then she stood up to work out where the entrance might be.

'All right, good dog, keep still, I'm coming,' she said, taking a few slow paces backwards. Yes! She'd judged correctly; the hole was at her feet.

Stretching out flat once more, Mandy peered into the tunnel-like entrance. The dog wasn't too far in, only about a metre or so; Mandy could just make out its back end. She'd have to try and get a really good grip round its body. If it struggled too much she'd have to pull as hard as she dared. She couldn't risk the dog going forwards; then it could be lost underground for ever.

'Slowly . . . careful now . . .' Mandy spoke softly and encouragingly, as much to herself as to the dog. Then she spluttered as she felt grains of dry soil around her lips and up her nose.

Her face and head were right inside the hole now, her arms and hands straining to get her closer. If she couldn't reach the dog, she'd have to wriggle out and find something to dig with. But . . . one more straining effort and Mandy's hands touched the dog.

Mandy managed to put her hands round its body. She pulled gently at first; nothing seemed to be happening. She pulled a bit harder; the dog didn't wriggle at all. It wasn't making a sound. Mandy was worried.

There was nothing else for it. Mandy heaved with all her might, using her feet to make herself move backwards at the same time.

Success! She'd got it! Slowly now, Mandy drew the dog out of the hole. 'Oh, no!' she murmured, staring worriedly at the little dog lying still and silent in her hands. What if the dog was dead?

Eleven

The dog was a Lakeland terrier, a female, wearing a collar, Mandy observed, as her hands moved quickly down the dog's mouth and nose to wipe away any earth.

'Ouch!' No question now. The dog was alive. Alive enough to have bitten Mandy's finger quite hard. She turned the little dog round to face her, and kneeled there with it in her arms. 'There, girl, you're all right,' Mandy soothed. 'Everything's all right.' The dog whined, wriggled her black curly body against Mandy's and reached her head up to lick Mandy's face.

'There, there,' smiled Mandy, looking at the

name disc on the dog's collar. 'There, there, Rosie. I know you didn't mean to bite me. You were frightened, weren't you, girl? And I must have hurt you, heaving you out like that. Come on, let's get us both back to Animal Ark!'

'She's called Rosie,' Mandy told her dad, as she hurried into the treatment room. 'Her breath smells a bit funny,' she added with a grimace, as Adam Hope stroked the little dog before lifting her from Mandy's arms.

'Well, apart from being hungry and thirsty, I think she's OK,' Mr Hope said after a quick examination.

'There's a phone number on her name disc,' said Mandy.

'Right,' said Mr Hope, placing Rosie on the treatment table. 'Leave her to me, Mandy, and go and get cleaned up.'

Mandy opened her mouth to protest then suddenly realised how dirty she and her clothes were. 'I'll see you later, Rosie,' she murmured, stretching out a hand to stroke the dog's head.

'Mandy?' demanded Mr Hope, pointing to her finger. 'Did Rosie bite you?'

'It wasn't her fault, Dad. I—'

'Go and wash yourself then get your mum to look at that bite. Now, Mandy! And no arguing.'

'OK, I'm on my way.'

Mandy hurried off to wash and change, carefully transferring the bits of antler to the pocket of her clean jeans. Then she went to find her mum to get her finger dressed.

'It will be a bit tender for a while, Mandy,' said Emily Hope. 'The skin's broken, but it isn't a very deep bite. Fortunately you had that anti-tetanus booster a couple of months ago.'

'It wasn't Rosie's fault,' Mandy said again. 'She was frightened and I hurt her a bit when I pulled her out. She's a lovely little dog. Has anyone got in touch with her owner yet?'

'Jean's seeing to it.' Emily Hope secured a plaster firmly in place. 'There, that should be all right. Yes, go on. Go through to the surgery and see what's going on.'

Mandy grinned. 'Thanks, Mum,' she said as she hurried away.

'Rosie's owner, a Mr Dickenson, is on his way,' Jean reported a minute later. 'Apparently Rosie has been missing over a week.'

'So it must have been her Gran and Grandad saw on the allotments,' said Mandy.

'Mr Dickenson has had search parties out. He informed his local police, put notices in his local shop windows . . .'

'Where does he live, Jean?' asked Mandy.

'Glisterdale,' the receptionist replied. 'Over twelve miles away! He's no idea how or why Rosie came to be in Welford. He thinks she must have got out by wriggling under a gate, but more than that he can't work out.'

'Incredible!' said Mandy. 'I'll go and see how she's doing.'

'Oh, and Lydia Fawcett phoned,' said Jean. Mandy stopped in mid-stride. 'She says you and James can go up to High Cross as soon as you like. Those two billies of hers, now what are their names . . . ?'

'Houdini and Monty,' said Mandy quickly, her heart sinking. 'What about them, Jean? They haven't attacked Sprite, have they?'

Jean shook her head and smiled. 'According to Lydia, they seem to have taken to the little fawn and are mothering, or should I say fathering, her!'

'Great!' said Mandy. Then her faced dropped. 'Oh, heck! James won't be able to come. He won't be back from York 'til late.'

Mandy spent a little while petting and fussing over Rosie, then showed her dad the pieces of antlers she'd found.

'Let's hope they help,' he said. 'Your mum went to see Sammy again and she isn't too happy about him at all!'

'I'll take them round now,' said Mandy. 'And then I'll go straight up to High Cross. Goodbye, Rosie. Your master will be here soon. I'll see you later, Dad.'

Mandy hurried out of the treatment room and through Reception. She'd almost reached the door to go out when it opened and a tall, friendly-looking man hurried in. 'I'm Peter Dickenson,' he said. 'I've come for Rosie. How is she? Is she all right?'

'I'll take you through,' said Mandy, warming to Mr Dickenson immediately. 'Dad has been checking her over but there didn't seem to be much wrong with her. I'm afraid I bruised her back a little bit when I pulled her out of the rabbit hole, though.'

Mandy opened the door to the treatment room and stepped quickly back as Rosie shot out yapping happily and made straight for her master.

Peter Dickenson bent to pick her up; the two

were obviously delighted to see each other;
Mandy swallowed hard as she watched the
reunion.

'You naughty girl!' laughed Mr Dickenson.
'How on earth did you get so far away from
home? And what have I told you about going
down rabbit-holes, hmm?'

'She obviously found food and drink,' said
Adam Hope, who'd come out to join them.
'There's no sign of dehydration. Just sore paws
and a bruised back.'

'What about her breath, Dad? Rabbits?' asked
Mandy.

'I think I can explain that smell,' Mr Dickenson told them. 'I'm afraid there'll probably be a very angry greengrocer somewhere around here. If I'm not mistaken, and I don't think I am, Rosie's found a supply of onions. She's got a thing about onions! She'll go to any lengths to steal them. For playing with and for eating, I'm afraid. She probably carried them off one by one and then hid or buried them. Could be she hid them down the rabbit-hole.'

'The Bedfordshire Champion!' Mandy and her dad spoke together, then laughingly explained to Peter Dickenson.

'You must give me his address and I'll go round and apologise,' said Mr Dickenson. 'Prize onions, Rosie! You've really done it this time, girl.'

'Well, I'm glad she's all right anyway,' said Mandy, patting Rosie and smiling. 'And now I'll go over to Ernie's.'

'Wait!' said Peter Dickenson. 'I haven't even thanked you yet.'

'It's OK,' said Mandy, anxious to be off. 'It was just lucky I was in the forest at the right time. And you've solved the mystery of the missing onions. Grandad will be so pleased it wasn't someone trying to wreck his friend's chances of winning a prize – and that he and Gran won't have to spend another night trying to catch a thief!'

Ten minutes later Ernie Bell and Mandy were standing by Sammy's run. Ernie was more than willing to see if Sammy would eat the deers' antlers.

'Shall we try him with the bigger piece first?' Mandy suggested, holding it out for Ernie to take from her.

'You call him over and give it to him,' Ernie said gruffly. But almost before he'd finished speaking, the squirrel bounded forward, scampered up the wire and jumped on to one of the supports. He chattered urgently, his eyes on the bit of antler in Mandy's hand.

And when Mandy held it out to him, Sammy almost snatched it away from her. He went up on his haunches, put his front paws to his mouth and nibbled vigorously at the antler.

'Well, I'll be . . .' Ernie shook his head and gazed at Sammy.

Mandy laughed. 'He seems to be enjoying it,' she said. 'Let's hope it does him some good.'

'Time will tell,' said Ernie.

Mandy smiled and nodded. Then, leaving Ernie still gazing happily at Sammy, she cycled away. She was off to High Cross to hear about Sprite.

Twelve

'I've never ridden so fast up that hill before!' Mandy laughed breathlessly when she arrived at High Cross. 'I can't wait to hear what's been going on!'

'Well,' Lydia said with a smile, 'this morning at milking-time I decided to keep Lady Jayne waiting a while. I hadn't fed Sprite since two a.m. so she was pretty hungry. You get the idea? One hungry fawn, one goat needing to be milked.'

'Crafty,' murmured Mandy. 'Did it work?'

'It was a bit of a gamble, really,' Lydia admitted. 'Lady Jayne would have been feeling pretty

uncomfortable and could really have turned on
Sprite. Anyway, I tempted Sprite out of her pen
by waving her feeding bottle around in front of
her nose.

'Keeping it just out of reach?' guessed Mandy
and Lydia nodded.

'She followed me into Lady Jayne's milking
pen,' Lydia went on. 'I managed to get Sprite
on one side of Lady Jayne and myself on the
other. Then I crouched down as if to start milking. I think Lady Jayne wondered where the
usual milking pail was, she seemed to be looking
for it. And, while Lady Jayne was busy looking,
I held Sprite's bottle next to her udder. Then I
squirted a drop of Lady Jayne's milk and pushed
her teat into Sprite's mouth instead of the teat
on the bottle.'

'Oh, Lydia!' said Mandy.

Lydia smiled. 'After that it was easy. Sprite
took her fill, wandered out of the pen and I
stripped the rest of the milk from Lady Jayne.'

'So Lady Jayne has accepted her!' Mandy said
happily.

'She wouldn't have anything to do with Sprite
afterwards,' said Lydia. 'Except to give her
haughty looks. But then Houdini and Monty

appeared. They'd climbed out of the walled
garden and came racing into the barn.' Lydia
shook her head, 'I thought I was in for big
trouble, I can tell you. I thought they'd go for
Sprite. It all happened so quickly I couldn't get
to her. But they greeted her like a long-lost
friend.'

'Oh, I do wish I could have seen it,' sighed
Mandy.

'Well, come on; now you've got your breath
back and heard most of the tale, we'll go and
see them. They're up in the enclosure.'

'How did you get Sprite up here?' Mandy asked
as they hurried to the top fields.

'Another gamble,' Lydia admitted. 'I got some
apples and carrots to make Houdini and Monty
follow me and just hoped they'd herd young
Sprite along with them.'

'And they did?'

'They did,' Lydia confirmed. 'They all came
into the enclosure and they've been there ever
since. I've checked on them from time to time,
but they completely ignored me. Houdini has
gone back to kid-hood, I think.'

'I see what you mean!' Mandy exclaimed in

delight. 'Just look at the three of them playing tag!' Mandy grinned, then sniffed and blinked hard.

Lydia gave her a quick hug. She knew exactly how Mandy was feeling. 'It does something to you, when things work out right, doesn't it!' she said softly. 'And it won't really matter if Lady Jayne won't let Sprite feed again. I can cope with bottle-feeding for a couple of weeks if I have to.'

But before Mandy went home, Lady Jayne allowed Sprite to suckle again. And, this time, she licked the little fawn while she was feeding.

Mandy called in at Lilac Cottage on her way home to give her grandparents all the news.

'We know about Rosie *and* her liking for onions, Mandy my love,' laughed Grandad.

'A nice fellow, that Mr Dickenson,' said Gran and Mandy smiled.

She spent a happy half-hour telling them all about Sprite and another happy half-hour telling her mum and dad when she got home.

The next three days passed all too quickly. Mandy and James had their holiday homework to finish, but they found time to go up to High

Cross and on Sunday evening, they went to see Sammy.

'He's almost as lively as usual!' James said as they watched the squirrel scamper to and fro.

'He certainly seems to have got over his twitchiness,' Ernie said, smiling when Sammy bounded over and stuck his paw through the netting for a piece of fruit. 'Those deers' antlers really seem to have put him right, Mandy!'

'They have, haven't they!' said Mandy.

The squirrel gave a little chattering bark. 'I think Sammy agrees!' said James with a laugh.

In the morning, before leaving for school, Mandy phoned Lydia. Then she cycled off to meet James at the Fox and Goose crossroads.

'Sprite's still happy and Lady Jayne's still letting her feed,' she told James when he arrived.

'Blackie's not too happy,' said James. 'He always gets the sulks the first school day after a holiday.'

'It was a good holiday,' Mandy smiled. 'And in two weeks we've got the WI Fete to look forward to. Oh gosh!' she added, 'there's Miss Davy. Apart from pinning a card and the photo on Animal Ark's board, I haven't done anything about finding a home for her friend's goldfish.'

'We can ask around at school,' said James.

When Mandy got home that afternoon, there was worrying news from High Cross. Sprite had somehow got out of the enclosure and had gone missing for over two hours.

'Lydia says Sprite found her own way back,' Emily Hope explained. 'But she's worried it might happen again. If Sprite made her way to the road she could get knocked down. Or cause a very nasty accident.'

'Or just get lost. And she can't fend for herself,' said Mandy in dismay. 'She could die of hunger or thirst if she wandered off again. Do you think she was trying to make her way back to the forest, Mum?'

'I don't know, love,' Emily Hope said gently. 'We'll just have to hope it doesn't happen again.'

Five days went by and Sprite didn't make any attempt to escape. But on Sunday morning Lydia phoned. Sprite had got out again, she'd been gone for three hours; and this time, Houdini and Monty were missing too! Lydia was as sure as she could be that they weren't anywhere on High Cross land.

'We'll go and search,' said Adam Hope, reaching for his keys. 'Come on, Mandy; we'll phone James from the mobile and pick him up on the way.'

Twenty minutes later, James and Mandy were peering anxiously out of the Land-rover windows. Mr Hope was driving slowly but they were nearly at Lydia's and they'd seen no sign of Sprite or the two billy-goats.

As they drove into the farmyard, Lydia ran towards them. 'They're back!' she shouted, as Mandy and James leaped out.

'Thank heavens for that!' sighed Mandy.

'Yes. But, Mandy, I'm beginning to wonder if we should think of something else for Sprite,' said Lydia. 'I've just had Sergeant Wilkins, the wild-life officer from police headquarters, on the phone. Sprite charged across the road right in front of his car. On the steep hill down to the village.'

'She's becoming a danger to herself and others, Mandy,' said Mr Hope. 'Lydia's right. We'll have to think of something else.'

'I don't know what!' Mandy sighed.

'Nor do I,' James agreed gloomily. 'But we'll try.'

'Maybe I should phone Gran and Grandad

and say we can't go with them,' said Mandy. Her
grandparents had invited her and James to go
for a drive out and a picnic lunch.

'I don't think that would do any good, Mandy,'
said Mr Hope. 'Besides, Gran will have the picnic hamper packed by now.'

'I'm not suggesting Sprite must go immediately,' Lydia said gently. 'I'm just asking you to
try and think of something.'

Although neither of them was really in the
mood for a picnic, James and Mandy managed
to enjoy themselves. And as they were driving
home, Gran suddenly pointed to a notice. 'Look,
there's an Open Day at Glisterdale Grange,' she
said. 'Let's call in. I've heard the gardens there
are beautiful.'

'There's a nature trail and forest walk,' said
James, as they drew up in a large forecourt. 'See,
Mandy! There's a big guide map just in front of
us.'

They all got out of the camper van and stood
looking at the guide map in its glass case. 'I
think we'd better let them go off on their own,
Dorothy,' said Grandad. 'We'll meet back here
in an hour, Mandy. All right?'

'James!' said Mandy a little while later. 'Wouldn't it be great if we could find somewhere like this for Sprite? This forest,' she waved her hands around, 'with other deer.'

'And goats and sheep down there in the paddocks,' added James.

'I wonder . . . ?' Mandy said thoughtfully.

'Uh-oh, I know that look. What have you thought of?' James asked.

'Well, we could just ask if we could see the owner,' Mandy said with a grin. 'Find out what he or she is like. And take it from there.'

'OK.' James agreed. 'Let's go to the office at the entrance. Someone there might tell us where to find the owner.'

So they hurried off and as they were walking up the path towards the entrance, a little dog barked excitedly and ran up to Mandy.

'It's Rosie!' said Mandy, stooping to stroke the little terrier.

'The dog you rescued from the rabbit-hole?' asked James.

'Yes. That's right. I hope she hasn't run away again. What is she doing here?'

'Hello, Mandy,' said an amused voice from behind them.

'Mr Dickenson!' gasped Mandy, straightening up. She introduced James to Rosie's owner.

'Do you work here?' Mandy asked in surprise.

'Well, actually, Rosie and I *live* here,' said Mr Dickenson. 'Glisterdale Grange is our home.'

James let out a soft whistle. And Mandy's surprise turned to something approaching shock.

'We were just coming to see if we could speak to the owner,' Mandy said after she had recovered. 'Except we didn't know it was you, of course.'

'But why, Mandy?' said Peter Dickenson. 'Why did you want to speak to me?'

'We'll have to explain from the beginning,' said Mandy. 'And it's quite a long story,' she added.

'Let's go into my study then,' said Peter Dickenson. 'We won't be interrupted there.'

So they went inside, and between them, Mandy and James told Mr Dickenson everything, right from the day they'd first found the little fawn lying in the forest next to her dead mother.

'And now she keeps escaping and we're terrified she'll either get lost and starve to death, or get knocked down like her mother did,' Mandy concluded.

'So you decided to ask me . . .' prompted Mr Dickenson.

'If . . . if it would be possible for Sprite to come here,' said Mandy. 'I don't think she'd *want* to escape from somewhere like this.'

'The trouble is,' said James, 'she would need a bit of looking after.'

'But you've got fallow deer in your forest,' Mandy said hopefully. 'Maybe they'd teach Sprite how to look after herself.'

'I've got something even better,' Peter Dickenson told them. 'I've a tame fallow doe I hand-reared three years ago. We call her Honey-Mum because she mothers everything. Puppies, kittens, foals, ducks . . .'

Mandy swallowed hard and gazed hopefully at him.

'I wanted to find a way of thanking you for rescuing Rosie,' Peter Dickenson continued. 'So I'd be more than willing to give your Sprite a home, Mandy. And with a fawn to look after, Honey-Mum would be in seventh heaven.'

'She's not weaned off milk yet,' said Mandy. 'But she will be in another week or so. I'm sure

Lydia will keep her until then.'

'Mandy, from what you've told me, I think the sooner Sprite comes here, the better,' said Peter Dickenson. 'I'd enjoy bottle-feeding her for however long she needs it.'

'I could ask Mum or Dad if they'd bring her tomorrow. After school, so James and I could come too,' said Mandy.

'It's only four-thirty. How about asking your parents and your friend at the goat farm if we could fetch the little fawn today after the Grange closes to the public?'

'Oh, brilliant!' cried Mandy, jumping to her feet. 'I'll phone them and Lydia and—'

'We'd better find your grandparents first, Mandy,' James pointed out.

'Gosh! I'd forgotten all about them!' Mandy gasped in dismay. 'They'll be wondering where we are, James!'

'I'll come with you and apologise to them for keeping you,' Mr Dickenson said, his eyes twinkling. 'I'm sure they'll remember Rosie, even if they don't remember me.'

Peter Dickenson organised everything remarkably quickly. By early evening Sprite and

Honey-Mum had been introduced and were happily getting to know each other.

'I can hardly believe it, James,' whispered Mandy. 'Look how Honey-Mum keeps darting forward then stopping to wait for Sprite.'

'Sprite hasn't taken her eyes off Honey-Mum since she first saw her,' said James.

'Happy, Mandy?' asked Adam Hope, ruffling her hair. He and Emily Hope had picked up Sprite at High Cross and driven her to Glister-dale in the Animal Ark Land-rover.

'Yes, Dad. I wish Lydia could have seen this, though. Look, they're lying down together now and . . .' Mandy sniffed, '. . . and Sprite's nuzzling Honey-Mum.'

'Mr Dickenson is going to make a video of it, Mandy. We'll invite Lydia over to Animal Ark to watch it one evening,' said Mrs Hope. 'We really should be getting back now.'

'All right,' Mandy agreed reluctantly. 'I know we'll see Sprite and Honey-Mum again. Mr Dick-enson said James and I could come over whenever we like. It's just this first time is so *special*.'

'I just wish we could be here the first time Sprite goes into the forest,' James said.

'Just think,' said Mandy, as Mr Dickenson's terrier bounded up to be stroked. 'If it hadn't been for Rosie here, none of this would have happened.'

After saying goodbye to Rosie, Mr Dickenson and Sprite, they drove back to Animal Ark. On the way home James grinned. 'You should have asked Mr Dickenson if he wanted some goldfish, too, Mandy!' he joked.

The goldfish problem was solved the next week at the WI Fete. Geoff, from the pet shop in Walton, had supplied a number of goods for the tombola stall which Mandy was helping to run alongside Gran.

Marion Timpson, a friend of Gran's and matron of the local cottage hospital, won a tub of goldfish food.

'I'll put it back for someone else to win,' she said. 'Goldfin, that old goldfish we had in pets' corner on the children's ward, died a couple of weeks ago.'

'You keep the food, Marion. I think Mandy can replace Goldfin for you,' Gran said in her no-nonsense voice.

'I didn't dare tell Matron there were three

goldfish,' Mandy chuckled to James later on. 'Now we've done our bit here, James, how do you fancy a long bike ride?'

'I wondered when you'd suggest that,' he replied. 'To Glisterdale, see how Sprite's getting on!'

An hour and a half later, Mandy was welcomed joyfully by Rosie. 'Here, Rosie,' said Mandy, 'I've brought you a present. An onion from your favourite allotment. Not a prize winner, I'm afraid,' Mandy added, laughing up at Peter Dickenson. 'But highly commended, which is better than nothing. Grandad and his friend are quite pleased about it anyway.'

Peter Dickenson laughed as well, then led them round to the paddock at the side of the house. 'That's strange,' he said. 'Honey-Mum and your Sprite were here a few minutes ago.'

'They're there,' said Mandy pointing. 'Look, on that little path that leads to the forest.'

'Follow them,' Peter Dickenson suggested. 'But don't get too close and don't make a noise.'

'Honey-Mum's behind Sprite now . . .' Mandy whispered a few minutes later. 'They're nearly at the start of the forest.'

'Sprite can't make up her mind what to do,'

James whispered back. Mandy could see that the fawn had stopped by the first lot of trees.

'Honey-Mum's stopped, too,' said Mandy. 'She's waiting to see what Sprite's going to do.'

Suddenly, Sprite pranced forward and disappeared behind the trees. But after a while she reappeared and pranced back to Honey-Mum. The doe nuzzled the little fawn, then they both lowered their heads to graze.

After a little while, Sprite started to move forward, towards the trees.

'Honey-Mum will glance up in a second,' Peter Dickenson told them. 'She'll want to make sure the little fawn is within sight.'

Honey-Mum did glance up. She followed Sprite, past the trees bordering the forest . . . up the slope to the forest itself . . . and . . .

'Sprite's out of sight,' sighed Mandy.

'They'll come back after they've explored for a while,' said Peter Dickenson.

'At last,' said Mandy, her eyes shining, 'our fawn is finally back in the forest!'

'And from now on she'll be able to go there whenever she likes,' James added happily.

The Animal Ark Newsletter

Would you like to receive The Animal Ark Newsletter? It has lots of news about Lucy Daniels and the Animal Ark series, plus quizzes, puzzles and competitions. It is published three times a year and is free for children who live in the United Kingdom and Ireland.

If you would like to receive it for a year, please write to:
The Animal Ark Newsletter,
c/o Hodder Children's Books,
338 Euston Road, London NW1 3BH,
sending your name and address
(UK and Ireland only).

ANIMAL ARK SERIES
LUCY DANIELS

All Hodder Children's books are available at your local bookshop or newsagent, or can be ordered direct from the publisher. Just tick the titles you want and fill in the form below. Prices and availability subject to change without notice.

Hodder Children's Books, Cash Sales Department, Bookpoint, 39 Milton Park, Abingdon, OXON, OX14 4TD, UK. If you have a credit card you may order by telephone – (01235) 831700.

Please enclose a cheque or postal order made payable to Bookpoint Ltd to the value of the cover price and allow the following for postage and packing:
UK & BFPO – £1.00 for the first book, 50p for the second book, and 30p for each additional book ordered up to a maximum charge of £3.00.
OVERSEAS & EIRE – £2.00 for the first book, £1.00 for the second book, and 50p for each additional book.

Name ....

Address ....

....

....

If you would prefer to pay by credit card, please complete:
Please debit my Visa/Access/Diner's Card/American Express (delete as applicable) card no:

Signature ....

Expiry Date ....